I0686875

IT DOESN'T HURT TO BE NICE

Text and Illustrations by

Amisha Sethi

Srishti
PUBLISHERS & DISTRIBUTORS

Srishti Publishers & Distributors
Registered Office: N-16, C.R. Park
New Delhi – 110 019
Corporate Office: 212A, Peacock Lane
Shahpur Jat, New Delhi – 110 049
editorial@srishtipublishers.com

First published by
Srishti Publishers & Distributors in 2015

Text © Amisha Sethi, 2015
Illustrations © Amisha Sethi, 2015

10 9 8 7 6 5 4 3 2 1

*This book is dedicated to the divinity of
every single person I have met in my life.
Thank you for being there for me.*

You are what your deep driving desire is,
As your desires, so are your thoughts,
As your thoughts, so is your will,
As your will, so are your deeds,
And as your deeds, so is your destiny.

—*Vedanta*

Acknowledgments

This book could not have been possible without the gorgeous presence of each and every person that came into my life to add value, and to give me experiences that are unique and beautiful.

I would like to acknowledge team Srishti for believing in the purpose of writing this book, and for their amazing support on every little nuance leading up to the final book.

I would like to thank Manoj Karthikeyan for believing in my dream and helping me at various stages of writing this book.

I would also like to thank my sister Shifali , my husband Kshitij, and a few special friends who read the portions of the book to give me honest feedback and positive motivation.

I would like to thank all my friends who relentlessly believed in me and went through countless conversations about how my book was shaping up.

I would like to thank Soundhariya and Vivek from Axiom who helped in every way to bring this book to your hands.

Finally, each and every person in my family who has loved me unconditionally and encouraged me to keep writing, no matter what.

Prologue

It was a hot and sunny afternoon in the month of February in 2014. I was sitting on a brand new chair; there were still bits of polythene on the handgrip. Around me was a group of twenty-five odd animated colleagues. Amidst total chaos, I was in total harmony – in peace, and filled with undiluted calmness – experiencing a nearly silent mind.

The day had finally arrived when I was to resign from one of the most coveted corporate positions in the country. In hindsight, the year leading up to this day had undoubtedly been the best time of my life. I don't say this about my professional life, but in every little sense about my spiritual one. Life is a bucket full of experiences; some are strange, some enthralling, and some just leave you gasping for breath.

These experiences of a lifetime made me, in simple words, a much better person than I had ever been. I love my new avatar which is much closer to the real 'me'. The magnificent writings from ancient Indian sages call it 'satya' or the truth.

I, Kiara Seth, a thirty-three-year-old corporate honcho was about to fly – not to another level or a bigger brand, but to take the biggest flight of my life. I had realized the purpose of my life, and with folded hands I had surrendered myself to the supreme truth.

Introduction

I am the richest, if my heart is full of kindness.

Here is a humble attempt to offer awareness about the power which each one of us possesses – the supreme truth, the ultimate universe. The medium is anecdotes – certain hilarious, enlightening and dramatic events from Kiara's life, combined with teachings from our ancient sages, philosophers and leaders who have tried spreading love, happiness and peace across our planet tenaciously. Kiara's brush with the 'truth' might appear disconnected from our individual realities, but the allusion is that we are all the same. We are one universal soul connected not just through Facebook, LinkedIn and Twitter of the man-made world, but by the basic facts of life: *evolution, love* and *purpose*. Our ancient texts, right from the Upanishads, flash the luminous light of wisdom effortlessly.

We come from Brahman (the fullness, the inexhaustible),
we go back to Brahman; in each one of us there is Brahman.

Here is an attempt to put forward inspirations drawn from ancient Indian spiritual knowledge that has been around for thousands of years. The timeless wisdom from the glorious Vedas which advocate the transcending values of grace, kindness, love, trust, faith and resilience are more relevant in today's materialistic world than ever before.

Amidst the mindless race for money and power, it incites us to take a second look at attractions and illusions called '*moh*' and '*maya*', and inspires in us thoughts of living life in utmost pleasure and peace.

It makes us take a good look at our lives, thoughts and progression. Do we need to step up, not just technologically from one gadget to another, but spiritually as better human beings who contribute to the betterment of society?

The basic requirement of humanity is to be civilized and civilizations can never evolve or grow without humans standing up and working together for the betterment of all.

Our lives seem like motion pictures produced and directed by God, where you play your character and everything else around you is scripted by a supernatural power. For your performance in the movie called *Life,* all you need to do is to be human and enjoy every experience that comes your way.

Oh God!

Each one of us has our own set of unique experiences related to the concept of God, religion and its corresponding beliefs. These beliefs are usually conditioned over a period of time based on the culture, family and the place you are born into. Pretty much none of these things are under your control at the time of your birth. So quite automatically and naturally, you pick up the culture, religion and beliefs of your family and social surroundings. In the early years of life, you are mostly immersed in the conditioning of loving and treating everyone around you with the same respect and reverence that you give to your family and close friends, no matter where they come from or what culture they belong to.

I'm not sure who introduced or popularized the trend of giving nicknames or pet names to children in India, but usually, the baby earns a love-name either a few hours after coming into the world, or in about a week's time. The names mostly fall into an inexplicable category; they are strange, meaningless and sometimes embarrassing. It's a uniquely Indian experience when ten-day-old Pappu, Munna or Chinku grow up into handsome, well-groomed men called Sid, Abhay or Ronit, but are addressed by the people around them – read relatives and childhood friends – by these embarrassing labels in front of anyone and everyone.

August 1980, Delhi

My parents, with great pride, gave me an additional nickname 'Baby'. And I, like any good toddler, used to chuckle sweetly every time anyone called me by this name. For a good part of my life, I was known to my entire family and friends as 'Baby'. From a little baby to being called Baby didi to Baby masi...the experience was somewhat dampening.

I always felt that my parents could have done a better job or at the least could have been a little more thoughtful while deciding on my nick name. Little did I know, however, that over thirty years later, in the city of chilly winds – Chicago – every bit of me would yearn to be called by my nickname.

As a child, you are somewhat closer to the truth. The madness of the materialistic world has not yet infiltrated your pure mind and heart with unnecessary feelings and emotions. You don't get carried away with so called manifestations of happiness: plenty of money, a big house, a BMW 5 Series car, a great figure, pimple-free skin, above eighty percent in exams, a super rich lover, a Versace dress, parties, super expensive alcohol on a dry day, job in an MNC, the latest smartphone, branded clothes, etc.

My earliest encounter with God dates back to 1985. I was four years old at the time and my grandmother used to recite the Gayatri Mantra to me every day. It was supposed to keep me away from all evil and also help me achieve all that I desired by wooing the Godhead.

ॐ भूर्भुव: स्व:
तत्सवितुर्वरेणियं।
भर्गो देवस्य धीमहि
धियो यो न: प्रचोदयात्।।

Om bhur bhuvah svah
tát savitúr várenyam
bhárgo devásya dhimahi
dhíyo yó nah pracodáyat

The Gayatri Mantra is a highly revered mantra from the Vedic tradition. Like all Vedic mantras, the Gayatri Mantra is thought to be authorless and is believed to have been revealed to the Brahmarshis. This is a Vedic Sanskrit verse from a hymn of the *Rigveda*.

Amusingly, I truly realized and followed the real meaning of one of the most powerful mantras of Vedic literature, twenty-eight years later at a pub in Los Angeles. I am going to talk about this in the chapter called 'Light Within' and will describe how I was exposed to the real beauty of the Indian scriptures.

My grandma is one of the strongest and most progressive women of her age. Her beauty lies in her perseverance and an absolutely serene nature; it is as if nothing can ever bring a tear to her eyes. The only time I have ever seen her cry was at Grandpa's funeral. But even at that time, astonishingly, she was the first one to take charge of the situation and get all of us back into a routine the very next day.

As I was growing up, she relentlessly told me, 'Baby, always do good deeds and never do anything against your conscience.'

There was a black and white list of 'to do' things, nicely packaged under the brand name 'sanskar' by my overtly religious family. To top it, I created my own farm fresh concept of a 'God bank' with a balance sheet of good and bad karmas.

My piggy bank was quickly filling up with karmas – both good and bad. I safely presumed that the dreaded Yama – god of death as per the Indian mythology – was keeping a sentient account of all my sins. Yama most likely would have kept chronicles of the numerous times I had slapped my younger brother whenever he troubled me while I was playing.

Until I reached puberty, I lived more in fear than with love for God. If I cheated during my exams, I would be punished by God; if I lied, God would take away all my toys; and if I thought badly of someone, then something terrible would happen to my parents (courtesy the main course of the delicious mythological stories told by my Grandma). The list of terrifying reasons to be a 'good girl' could go on.

The most frightening of the lot was that if the number of sins became greater than the good deeds, the demons would make nice pakoras of you and fry you in hot boiling oil once you die. You might be barbecued or grilled as well, I guess, depending upon the demons' mood.

One sleepy afternoon, when I was in standard nine in the autumn of 1993, I was surfing the channels on our old TV and praying hard that the cable operator would broadcast a Hollywood film. (It was nearly a rare cosmic event if he showed a recent English movie.) The cable operator certainly despised English movies, and the ones he liked (anyone's guess), he devotedly showed between midnight and 2.00 a.m. In the midst of my fervent prayers, my father suddenly caught me off guard by handing me a flyer about Swami Vivekananda. It was an invitation to a seminar and before I could throw it away to destroy any chances of attending, a simple verse caught my eyes. It has lived with me from then on:

Three Golden rules of life,
Who is helping you, don't forget them,
Who is loving you, don't hate them,
Who is trusting you, don't cheat them...

I was indeed aware of Swami Vivekananda as an Indian Hindu monk (born in 1883 in India) who played a key role in introducing the Indian philosophies of Vedanta and Yoga to the world. I learned about him and his glorious work from our short, plump and visibly enthusiastic history teacher who indefatigably praised Swami Vivekananda as a torch bearer in raising higher levels of self-awareness and spiritual wisdom not just in India but also in the western world.

It goes without saying that I never attended the seminar and the cable operator played *Indecent Proposal* that evening. The movie had a passionate kiss totally worth the wait. Such racy films were a big deal back then but the simple lines of that seminar invitation played over and over in my mind... refusing to go away. Without even realizing when, I started implementing them in my day-to-day life events.

●

No one has ever attained God by being in fear. Only when we free ourselves of fear, can the beauty of our actions demonstrate the cosmic fruit of results.

> ❤ *Do things not because of a fear of God or any kind of pressure, but to grow the fruits of love, trust and truth.*

I spent a considerable part of my childhood fearing the most beautiful creations of God. Each of God's creations is so astonishingly mystical in its own way. Thanks to the spiritual inclination in the later part of my life, I am today nearly unscathed by fears about doing things or of worshipping God because of some conceivable fear. Life has to be about living every day, every moment with utmost desire, energy and love. An inexorable belief that God is present in the smallest of creations around you – from a little insect to a magnificent bird to every human being on this planet – indeed makes you feel that God is everywhere; in each one of us. The only way to reach him is to love all and fear nothing.

I chose to believe the ancient sages, who in turn taught that our 'self' or the '*atman*' resides in each living being as an immortal soul (pure consciousness) that never dies; it just changes its form from one body to another, just like we change our clothes. And the one who attains the 'self', reaches the Godhead, the supreme power, the power of a thousand suns!

Life is like a boomerang where each released vibration, positive or negative, comes back to you in the same form of energy. If you release positive energy using speech or actions or even thoughts, the same comes back to you, not necessarily from the same person, but from thousands of others. Let this positive energy be for the betterment of everyone around you, and not just yourself. After all, when you pray for everyone, that is indeed the time you truly pray to God.

Visual representation from the 1903 edition of the Mahabharata

Thousands of years ago, Lord Krishna taught Arjuna this immortal wisdom, the supreme truth and art of living in the midst of an epic war. This was soulfully captured as endearing slokas in the *Bhagavad Gita*. The spiritual knowledge in the *Bhagavad Gita* is not only unique and timeless but it also indicates the path to achieving the ultimate purpose of your life.

Lord Krishna inspires Arjuna by saying:

Free yourself from the fear of me, the fear of seeing me in intergalactic form!
I am in every form both material and living, only a still mind with peace at heart can attain me,
Those whose minds are fixed in me in total faith,
He who hates none, he who has no envy or ego,
He who is kind, full of love, graceful, compassionate,
Stays the same in happiness and sadness,
He who is forbearing, masters his thoughts,
Unattached to fear and anxiety is dear to me,
Those who are dear to me, reach me.

Give Unconditionally

When you give, you get.
If the input is not with 'selfless intentions', the output can never be right.
Give unconditionally to receive unconditionally.

If you have ever given genuinely to someone – not a sacrifice because that is just suppressing one's own desires – but truly giving to someone with selfless intentions, you can feel the genuine elevation. There is an aura which is so pure and peaceful that you want to remain soaked in that very moment all your life.

When you ask for happiness, try to ask not just for yourself, but for everyone. Can you imagine how amazing you would feel if someone out there is secretly wishing you bliss and hoping that all your desires are getting fulfilled by the universe in abundance.

The one who only takes and never gives is a thief. You don't have to be a robber; give selflessly to get in abundance. The best thing you can ever give to anyone is blessings; the blessings of happiness, well-being, prosperity and even food.

> ♥ *Giving also means not just giving something to someone, but also giving yourself freely – to be submerged in the flow of life without rationalizing every turn and path taken.*

It was a hot summer in 1997 and the results of the engineering entrance exams were out. I scored an all-India rank of 3500. I could now easily get admission to the top engineering colleges of India, albeit only outside Delhi. Unfortunately, I couldn't clear either DCE or IIT Delhi.

I mustered up the courage to tell my Dad to send me to Roorkee, Manipal, Chandigarh or Bangalore, or if I were lucky, to Pune. Dad looked at me as if I had asked him to send me to Europa, one of Jupiter's moons!

He didn't speak much; he just responded with simple but firm lines:

'Baby, I suggest you get yourself enrolled in BSc Electronics or Maths honours in Delhi University. We don't want you to be away from us. You know Chikoo's condition. Your mom and I are going through a tough time now and we want you around.'

I felt a strong, selfish urge to reply harshly,

'No! I *want* to go. What the hell? I am not a baby who can't live alone. And it's not my problem if my younger brother has Down's Syndrome. Why do I have to suffer because of it? I want to go out, enjoy hostel life, have boyfriends, experience night outs and above all, I am not a moron who burnt the midnight oil solving monster physics numericals to end up here at home as your private entertainer.'

Before I could vent out the anger and frustration my intellectual mind was reeling under, I suddenly heard a voice deep down.

Don't hurt those who love you...

So after a long pause, and knowing full well the implications of what I was going to say, I finally said, 'Sure, Papa. I understand.'

I gave in to my parent's wishes and they deserved every bit of my capitulation. There was no sacrifice involved in my action here because I was never interested in engineering in the first place. Just that it sounded cool to be an engineer and I knew I could pull it off.

And what I received in turn was absolutely phenomenal. Those three years in Delhi University became the best years of my life, thanks to a conducive environment, some great friends and happy parents.

I unfailingly participated in every possible event, dance competitions, dramatics, and choreography. I even learned different kinds of dance forms. The journey was so enriching that by the end of my three years, I didn't want to leave DU.

I made friends for life; these people became my biggest support system and I know I am theirs. DU days were all about masti, dance, fun with friends, having a gala time and bunking classes. During those fun-filled days, I also found out that Dad had been suffering severe losses in our manufacturing business that dealt with magnets and magnetic products.

I remember going to his office on random days and chatting endlessly on Yahoo! Messenger with my old school gang.

I was a queen in my Dad's office, with the staff gathering around me with an unlimited supply of samosas, tea, sandwiches and juices whenever I visited. Till then, I had never realised how happy my parents were about the fact that I was around when they were going through the toughest phase in their lives. Gladly, I hadn't listened to my intellectual mind but to the feeble sound of that quiet voice.

Later, in 1999, during a lazy winter afternoon at my Dad's office, Dad caught me off-guard. I had taken my usual table in his office which had a spare computer with an Internet connection. That was all I needed for the much-needed everyday chat session with my school gang. Since this bunch of friends lived with the motto 'live and laugh every second', I was very fond of them all.

'Hey guys! How about a movie on a private big screen?' I announced.

'Got to be *Vaastav*,' Ronik is the first one to reply. Ronik is the chocolate boy of our group, fair and cute, has chubby cheeks but also a pot full of hard luck. For some reasons (that he hasn't been able to crack as yet), he could never make a girlfriend. Once a universal brother, always a default brother to all girls, including myself. I am sure he hated the word 'brother' more than anything in this world.

'*Reshma ki Jawani Jungle Mein*.' Bang came Sid's reply, quickly followed by a grinning-devil icon.

We could actually imagine his naughty face even without being on a video chat. Sid, the stud, the very *jaan,* the sweetheart of our group. But there was a problem with his luck too. Despite being so amazingly charming and good looking, he was never lucky in areas like love, entrance exams, his relationship with his father, etc. But God had compensated for all that by giving him an absolutely crackling sense of humour in abundance. I used to get along with Sid like a fish to water. We used to laugh non-stop on every word possible, and sometimes after our laughter attack, we even used to forget why we had started laughing at the first place!

I snapped smilingly at Sid, 'Oh god, Sid! when will you grow out of Reshma's Jawani?'

'It feels awesome to analyze Reshma on a big screen.'

Simmi distracted Sid promptly with her submission, 'Has to be *Something about Mary,* and I prefer Cameron any day over Reshma madam.'

I gave my choice, as usual a romantic movie. I so wanted to find my soul mate soon, but for now was happy and content in watching soul mates mating...*ahem,* I mean meeting on a movie screen.

'How about *Shakespeare in Love?*'

Ronik revolted, 'English movies bore me to death. It's got to be *Kuch Kuch Hota Hai.*'

Sid responded in a flash, 'To enjoy something, one needs to understand it! 'What about *Species*?'

'Dude, you understand only with the sub titles,' Ronik typed in.

Simmi didn't like the idea perhaps. 'Not *Species*, please.'

Simmi, the cute babe, my 2.00 a.m. friend, always helpful, pure as gold and amazingly dumb. I am sure she even used to mug up the name of the exam before appearing for it. I always used to wonder about her mugging and cooking capabilities. All said and done, she was the most sorted person in the group. She wanted to get married as soon as possible and get rid of this 'study and career *siyaapaa*' stress sooner than later.

I finally gave my verdict like a self-appointed group leader. 'OK guys, stop fighting! It's a done deal, the final choice is *There's Something About Mary* and we are gonna watch it at Sid's place two weeks from now. I am going to get a projector from Dad's Office.'

'You can count on me for food,' Simmi joined in excitedly.

Sid replied immediately thereafter, 'I will get beer for all of us and milk for the Baby!'

'Sid, I will kill you if you call me baby ever again.' Well, so much for my love for my nickname.

'Ok Baby :)'

'Wait until I see you!!'

Ronik went into the Hindi romantic movie phase I guess, and typed emotionally, 'Can't wait to see you all!'

That's when someone from Dad's office came and told me he wanted to see me. 'Hey! dad is calling me. Gotta go. Love you guys. Bye!'

After a hurried goodbye, I logged out of the messenger, leaving behind a final yellow bright smiley.

My dad has a reputation of being strict. I think that comes from managing one's own business, having to deal with various kinds of people. So there are times when he looks like someone extremely tough to get along with, but everyone knows he has a heart of gold. His kind actions have spoken for him time and again, both within the family and at his workplace. He is one of those who look as hard as a rock on the outside, but are actually as soft as cream inside.

He assumed the same serious look that has sent many in his office scurrying away and asked me inquisitively, 'Kiara, what have you planned to do after college?'

As usual, I had not seen this coming, and wasn't ready for Dad's heavy-duty questions. My mind started rebooting the system which was completely occupied with an extremely important discussion that I'd just had on movies. My mind

Googled and gave back a few top line search results to Dad's query, none of which had been thought out thoroughly.

'Maybe you can marry me off to a super-rich handsome dude from your business circle,' I said.

'Well in that case, I have a boy in mind,' said Dad quite seriously.

Are you kidding me?

'Dad! What's wrong with your sense of humour? I am not sure, but maybe choreography.'

'Do you want to join a group of dancers...the kind that dance behind actors?' said Dad and started laughing.

A little embarrassed, I clarified, 'No papa, choreographers are the ones who teach these actors how to dance.'

'Oh, okay okay! So do you see any scope money-wise?' Dad asked, though still laughing.

'No, not really. I may have to struggle for a few years in Mumbai before I can land a job somewhere. But before that, it would be great if I can go to the Broadway Dance Centre, New York for a special one year course in technical skills.'

'Well, I don't think we can afford New York. And I don't think we would want you to be so far away. What about an MBA?' he said, with a sharp gaze.

I started thinking aloud: I don't want any kind of financial or emotional burden on my parents; an MBA is something I should think of, though not sure why. I can at least make some decent money if the choreography idea doesn't work. I can pursue my passion along with MBA and also stall any possibilities of marriage for the next two years.

'I understand! MBA is definitely an option. I will start the preparations, 'I said.

I was lost in thought about this conversation back home in the evening. Coincidentally, someone sent me an SMS that said: *If things are going your way, it is good. But if they are not, relax because it's going God's way.*

Says Bhartrihari, a fifth century Sanskrit poet in his mesmeric writings:

परिभ्रमसि किं व्यर्थं क्वचन चित्त विश्राम्यतां
स्वयं भवति सद्यथा तत्तथा नान्यथा।
अतीतमपि न स्मरन्नपि च भाव्यसङ्कल्पय–
न्नतर्कितगमनाननुभवस्व भोगनिह।।

Paribhramasi kim vyartham kvachan chitta vishramyatam swayam bhavati tadyatha tat tatha na-anyatha. Ateetamapi na smarannapi cha bhaavya sankalpyanna tarkita gamanananu bhavasva bhoganih.

Oh Mind! Why are you always so restless; always wandering around? Please rest somewhere. Let the natural flow of life happen, as it cannot be changed. It is bound to happen. Therefore, enjoy the pleasures of now; forthcoming events and their going cannot be ascertained, without remembering what has already happened and without expecting anything of the future.

January 2000
On a lazy afternoon amidst Delhi's chilly winter, I was sitting with my DU gang outside PVR cinemas in Saket, discussing

what was next for all of us. We were all feasting on freshly-baked pizzas.

I heard Devina talking about an MCA course from a private institution in South Delhi. Devina was smart, logical and gorgeously hilarious. She was dating one of our classmates and had lofty dreams to marry him sooner than later.

My closest friend at that time, Gauri – studious with long golden hair – was busy discussing doing a Master's of Sciences and how she could make at least fifteen thousand rupees per month once she completed the course. Interestingly, Gauri had a secret crush on the same guy Devina was dating and that gave me ample opportunities to tease her all the time.

Komal was straight out of a painter's canvas when it comes to being a perfect girl. She was coy, yet full of life, an academic scholar and amazingly sweet. She was waiting for her boyfriend's plan so that she could navigate hers accordingly.

Ajay was busy texting his girlfriend that he was out with the guys and there were no girls around. I could see words coming out of his phone's keypad. *Trust me baby... What? Kiara?? Of course she is not here.*

Ajay was a sweet, naughty, not so academically sound guy. The kinds known as the typical Delhi university guys.

I was looking forward to my management entrance exam results. Though I still wanted to pursue a technical training course in dance, but almost paradoxically, I had found contentment and peace in my decision (on dad's recommendation of course) to pursue MBA too. Maybe that harmony had resulted from selfless giving in to the circumstances.

Back then, I was too naïve to understand the power of the universe, but as I now connect the dots, I am so glad that

I just went with the flow. The two years of my MBA degree at the Amity Business School changed my personality, my perception of life and most importantly, my confidence level. It made me fall in love with the subject 'Brand Marketing'. Even twelve years after leaving college, recollections about every single day spent in the beautiful campus in Noida fills my heart with utmost joy and gratefulness towards my extraordinary professors who relentlessly helped me acquire knowledge, and not just a degree; my friends who made each day a celebration; and my Dean, who told me on the day of convocation:

'A true leader never claims but distributes success. Don't ever forget that, Kiara, as you step out.'

Thanks to the kind words of my Dean, I had a unique set of values and principles even before I stepped into the corporate world.

Back at the Pizza Hub, a short and visibly cheerful waiter served our respective pizzas. The career discussions were on in full swing; so was the enjoyable munching of the hot steaming pizzas. I have usually been, by default, the only vegetarian across different groups of friends, colleagues and family, and the same was the case with this group too. As a result, I had an entire pan pizza to myself, which the others would surely dig into. When I was about to take the first slice, someone caught my attention. There was a sweet, crippled boy around eight years old, trying to scrounge some leftover food from the green dustbin next to the Pizza Hub.

I looked at him sympathetically and he smiled gently. I got up and gave my share of pizza, untouched, to the little boy. He accepted the food gratefully, and said softly. 'Thank you, didi.'

Ajay shouted, 'What's wrong with you, Kiara? You could have given it to me if you were not hungry.'

And I spontaneously replied (I'm not sure where this wisdom came from), 'I wanted to give it to him *because he is in need, not greed.*'

Later in the evening, I came out for my routine post-dinner walk. I was in my black track pants and newly-acquired blue Adidas jacket to keep me warm. Delhi winters are usually harsh, and dry cold can play a havoc on you. I decided to step out of the apartment complex and surprisingly started to walk towards the Shiva temple, not too far from my house. It was closed when I reached, but I noticed a weak and startlingly sick girl in her teens. She was leaning on to the temple wall and was shivering uncontrollably. She was wearing a cotton suit, with just a cotton shawl in the name of warm clothes, which was doing no good to her.

'Are you alright?' I asked her spontaneously.

'I have fever,' she could barely reply in her weak and low voice.

I looked around the nearby market and noticed all shops had been closed down for the day. Just one small tea shack opposite to the temple was open. I crossed the road and brought a tall glass of tea and bread to where the girl was sitting.

The girl started to sip the tea, and I could see she was slightly better, but was still shivering like someone under an epileptic attack. I was thinking how to comfort her.

'Take this. You will feel better,' I said while I removed my jacket.

'No, I can't take this,' she said sweetly.

'What is your name?' I said while I helped her slip in to my super warm jacket.

'Noori.'

I smiled, 'Noori, you need it more than anyone else. I anyways look fat in this jacket. It doesn't suit my figure at all.' I giggled naughtily, trying to cheer her up.

'Thank you!' she said in her giggling voice.

I started to run back to my house in a white cotton top that I was wearing under my ex-jacket. Now it was my turn to shiver!

I reached my house and rang the doorbell about five times. My grandmother opened the door and was completely shocked to see me like that.

'Where the hell is your jacket? What happened?' She started her 'caring' interrogation.

'Nothing dadi! Just gave my jacket to someone.'

'You gave your jacket to someone?? What is wrong with you?And in this three degrees Celsius, you are in this cotton top that too cut from sides and almost backless. Are you mad?' She was on a spree, scolding me sweetly, but seriously concerned.

'Dadi, just take a chill pill. I need to slip into my quilt or I will be your ice cube.'

My sister Ana was watching all this and asked me with her naughty smile, 'Where did you leave your jacket?'

I winked at her and half-laughingly told her, 'Don't tell anyone! I made out with this hot stranger whom I met behind the temple and forgot my jacket with him.' We both laughed out loud, knowing full well how unlikely that was.

'Yeah right, didi! You can do all that only in dreams. Good night and love you!' she said with a warm hug.

That night, before I fell into deep sleep, the faces of those two kids I had helped appeared before me and I felt an amazing gush of contentment and happiness that I had never felt before.

Mahatma Gandhi once said, 'The world has enough for everyone's need, but not enough for everyone's greed.'

I could easily relate to this great leader of the Indian subcontinent and felt pride in having adhered to one of his noble teachings.

From that day onwards, it became my standard ritual to offer fruits, bread and biscuits to the poor children at a Shiva temple near my house. They started calling me 'Achiwali Didi' (meaning, good sister) and they would share many stories about their dreams, schools and what they want to become once they grew up , etc., with me. I taught them a few English words and phrases like 'Thank You', 'Welcome', 'How are you?', 'Fine', 'No', 'Yes', 'Okay', 'Do it', 'Please give', 'God', 'May I' and 'Really', and they proudly used these words anywhere and everywhere, and sometimes all at once!

●

The spiritual teachings of the ancient Upanishads consider the giving of food as the most honorable donation.

The Upanishads are an expression of supreme truth that have come down to us along with the Vedas, the ancient and extremely sacred collection of hymns by wise and learned sages.

Though these scriptures hold within their pages complex knowledge and wisdom, in the simplest form it tells you to love all, because in each one of us there is a soul that never dies. That soul is Brahman, infinite and indivisible. This self, which is pure and with infinite opportunities, is deep down in the lotus of our heart and our biggest motto in life should be to achieve the self, the Lord of Love, the supreme, the Brahman. And undoubtedly, the path to achieving this higher consciousness and eternal peace is through unconditional giving.

I was quite inspired by the following centering on food in the *Taittiriya Upanishad*:

> *Respect food, give food, the body is made of food... Food and the body exist to serve the 'Self'.*
>
> *Don't waste food, water and fire... fire and water exist to serve the self. Grow more food; the earth can deliver food in abundance. Earth and space exist to serve the self.*
>
> *Refuse not food to the hungry, for when you feed the hungry, you serve the Lord.*

The $240 billion net income of the world's hundred richest billionaires would have ended poverty four times over, according to the Oxfam report released in 2013. Imagine: just a hundred people can eradicate extreme poverty from the world and feed the billions of hungry people on the planet.

Forget the billions...Can you attempt to feed just one person every day or week or month or even a year selflessly? One who is truly in *need*?

The fastest way to receive is to give, because giving starts the cycle of receiving. What we give, how much and to whom is undeniably the sole factor for determining what we receive. Give the best of yourself every day: smile, give food, give kindness, give love, and ultimately just give without any expectations...just for the sheer joy of it!

Interestingly – and I often wonder why people don't realise this – giving does not only refer to passing on something that belongs to you to someone who needs it more than you do. It also means giving yourself freely to the present moment. 'Now' is the only time which is truly yours and every time you give yourself unconditionally to 'Now,' life flows easily and brings to you amazing experiences which are beyond one's imagination.

One of the most essential ingredients of an enlightened living is to contribute selflessly to this life. When you do random acts of kindness (no matter what you give), your own life becomes richer. To nurture a meaningful life of serenity, joy and bliss, give your best to every moment, person or situation with utmost sincerity. Do not judge people on the basis of the bank balances they have but the space they have in their hearts. Make your heart the richest place on this planet with goodness and blessings for all. This attitude will take you to a wellspring of peacefulness, joy and open up boundless opportunities to grow.

> ♥ *Make this world a better place by starting with yourself and if at all you want to chase anything, chase the higher purpose of consciousness which is to give selflessly for the betterment of all.*

This beautiful ancient Vedic mantra has left me speechless with the choice of words and absolutely unconditional sense of giving of self for the betterment and peace of this universe.

ॐ द्यौ शान्तिरन्तरिक्ष: शान्ति: पृथ्वी
शान्तिराप: शान्ति औषधय: शान्ति:
वनस्पतय: शान्तिर्विश्वे देवा: शान्तिब्रह्मा

शान्ति: सर्व: शान्ति: शान्तिरेव शान्ति:
सामा शान्तिरेधि
ॐ शान्ति: शान्ति: शान्ति: ॐ।।

Om dyau shantih antarikshah shantih prithvi
shantiraapah shantih aushadhayah shantih
vanaspatayah shantih vishve devah shantibrahma
shantih sarvah shantih shantireva shantih
sa ma shantiredhi
Om shantih shantih shantih.

May peace prevail on earth, sky and the space everywhere
May peace reign all over this earth, in water and in all plants, trees and animals
May peace prevail all over the 'Brahman'
May peace be in the Supreme Being Brahman.
May we all coexist with peace, love and serenity always.
Peace, peace and peace to us and all beings!
Om shantih shantih shantih.

Try practising the essence of this ancient mantra as you embrace each new day and you will feel full of energy and vitality that can help you sail you through any challenges that might be lined up for you during the day.

Trust, Trust and Trust

There is only one way to reach the supreme truth, and it is to be the truth.
Trust the truth in self and all beings, as we all are same, we all are pure.

Inspired by Brihadaranyaka Upanishad
(Great forest of knowledge)

Trust is the basis of any relationship that one might have with animate and inanimate beings on this planet. You've *got* to trust in something...or rather everything: the inner self, people around, your destiny, the chain of events in your life, and above all, your conscience.

You trust that your car will not break down when you sit in it every single day; you trust that your friends will not poison your drink before offering it to you; you trust your parents to not leave you alone no matter what happens; you trust the air you are inhaling with the task of keeping you alive.

However, there are times when we become judgmental, saddled with myopic vision, and without realizing the power of self or of universal energy, we create barriers of dishonesty, eventually hurting ourselves and others. We start to mistrust our situations, our own people and get entangled in the never ending cycle of insecurities.

Trust is the foundation for peace, growth and evolution. The biggest enemy of trust is deceit and diffidence. When you start to fear or become insecure in a situation, or a person or simply the future, your neurotransmitters (read, mind) start to produce in you all kinds of false thoughts. It just pulls you away from your pure Self (the immortal and complete *aatman*, your own soul). The irony is that no matter how much the inner self tells you to trust the people and world around you, you end up not trusting them because of your self-produced 'garbage' thoughts.

Criminals commit crimes to rationalize their own thoughts, no matter how irrational they are. Evil is nothing but the absence of kindness and truth. The absence of truth occurs when we are psychologically not complete in ourselves and in the present moment. We become victims of our false imagination and assumptions of reality.

> ♥ One has to understand that there is a parallel reality for any path taken at a given point in time. And the closer you are to the truth in your actions, words and heart, the closer you are to your goal and absolute reality.

2003: My first job

High on energy and the passion to do well, I now entered the mean world of money. Anyone remotely aware of the corporate world and its working will understand what I mean.

Every day, I dressed up like a queen and sought my parents' blessings before leaving for office and sitting in my corner (no, no, not the corner cabin) workstation as if it was the God of Gods Indra's throne and I was ruling the biggest telecom giant with all-new ideas and unswerving passion. I had a fire in my belly to do well and I had just begun a romance with my boyfriend, who is now my husband.

'Hey! What's up lazy bum?' I spoke into my brand new Nokia phone. I had called my boyfriend during one of my coffee breaks in the office, to boast about my new marketing campaign with the excitement level of an astronomer who has just discovered life on an Exoplanet.

'Hey missing you. We haven't met for a week now,' responded Ram, tall, fair and amazingly good looking. The teenage boy I first met in 1995 had now grown into a handsome, immature and a crazy lover. He used to claim that he had fallen in love with me the moment he saw me. And I always used to laugh it off saying, 'Ya right, dude!'

I replied almost at the speed of light, 'Hey me too... but before that, you've got to hear this. I have cracked a campaign to increase revenues by at least twenty percent. This is cross marketing but in a completely new avatar where I have filtered database in such a way that the campaigns will be running only on segmented niche audiences intelligently identified for a set of products and services. Isn't that super cool?'

'Hmm...'

'What the hell? Just hmm? C'mon, Ram.'

Ram smiled, 'Forget this gyaan, Kiara. How about a kiss?'

I replied teasingly, 'That's so typical Ram! Yes, of course. Just sending you over data packets.'

Ram as usual got hassled about this whole chase over a mere kiss, 'God! Never date a marketer, especially one in a telecom company.'

I said playfully, 'Please don't. Okay, have to go now. Pick me up today at six sharp.'

I had no clue that this boasting about my 'amazing achievement', obviously only in my own eyes, was overheard by one of my senior colleagues who, without thinking or using any of his neurotransmitters efficiently, walked up to my CEO and complained that I was most likely passing databases on to my boyfriend who was apparently working on something that was competitive. All hell broke loose on my so-called Indra throne. I was flabbergasted and was called for a meeting with the CEO and the head of HR the very same day.

I knew I was in deep trouble. For some reason, Mahatma Gandhi's words resounded in my mind like a persistent note, 'Fear nothing if you haven't done anything wrong.'

I wanted my mind, heart or whatever to shut up because here I was, about to be fired on the grounds of cheating! I was barely six months old on the job and life couldn't have taken a more dramatic turn.

I entered the room, feeling as if I was choking with tension. I felt like a Russian spy caught by the FBI. The CEO asked me to hand over my mobile and started looking at the numbers. I wasn't sure what he was looking for because way back in 2003, we didn't even have an eight GB memory on mobiles to remotely store the database of one million subscribers.

The moment he questioned me, it was as if the Rani of Jhansi's spirit took over and, shivering with anger, I exploded. The fire in my belly came out of my mouth like a supernova.

'I haven't passed on any databases to anyone. It's merely a figment of someone's imagination. I am here to be the best brand marketer in India and I will become that sooner rather than later. If you want to believe me, do that; if not, I will be happy to leave right away. I am speaking the truth and nothing else.'

The HR head was listening to all this and abruptly asked me to stop and wait outside the room. I realised I was sweating profusely. A sudden silence engulfed the room. I wanted to shoot myself in the head for being so rude. The guy must have expected an apology for the kind of complaint that had been made against me, a pleading face at the least...and here I had almost hit back hard for daring to ask me this question.

After exactly fifteen minutes, I was called in and was told by my HR head that they believed me and asked me to get back to work.

And exactly a year later, I was given the best employee award by the same CEO. I am still in touch with him and thank him from the bottom of my heart for trusting me.

However, it was the HR head who apparently convinced the CEO to believe me. I will be grateful to him every single day that I live on this planet. Not because he helped me save my job, but because he taught me the biggest lesson of my life:

To trust relentlessly.

Rajan Singh Sodhi, the then HR head, tall, with a clear complexion, always wore a business suit with a matching tie and a turban. That day, he chose to believe in me when every other thing pointed against me. Not just that, in order to stand by me, he had to go against his own boss. He had faith in me, despite the fact that we were strangers. I asked him what had made him believe in me, and he simply said, 'Your eyes and a strong hunch.'

I call that hunch a '*shakti*', the faith, the trust which all of us have. This pure consciousness is present in each one of us and out of mere insecurities or greed, we let it go.

We stop believing in ourselves, our own friends, our parents, our colleagues and all other beings around us.

Imagine a world where we all trust each other; then there will certainly be no possibilities for wars between two people, states or countries.

The pure joy of being is in peace. This peace comes from a still mind; a mind which is not a production engine for 'junk thoughts'. I am proud of what I learned at an early stage of my corporate voyage. It's not that everyone around you is a saint and will not break or take advantage of your trust. But because of those few people teeming with negativities, one must not let go of such a powerful feeling of trust. And trust me, even if someone breaks your trust, at the end of the day, you will be content for having done the right thing by trusting unconditionally.

The *Bhagavad Gita,* one of the most beautifully written spiritual teachings in existence, says,

> '*The ones who break trust or are insecure, no matter how much they earn or gain in a short horizon, can never be a true yogi.*'

And by yogi, I don't mean an ascetic or someone proficient in yoga; it stands for a person who has attained self-realisation, who has become one with the godhead within. So do not be concerned with the outcome or with the fruits of your true actions. 'Karma Yoga' is about doing the right things without attaching yourself to the results. And once you are in this profound state of being, no matter what, you will trust and be trusted by others.

One can argue that it is difficult to trust what cannot be seen or understood. But anything that is not yet created in our eyes and physical form already exists in a super condensed form. Imagine a castle once in the form of a sand particle, or a little child in the form of a sperm and egg. It is no wonder that for a thousand years, wiser human beings believed in the power of imagination and not just mere knowledge.

Immerse yourself in the present moment. You will see all unhappiness, struggles, stress and insecurities dissolve.

The glorious authors of the Upanishads unfold the path of enlightenment through their profound wisdom:

'The marg of satya (the path of truth) and faith (an undiluted reverence for the Supreme Being) is the way to achieve and create everything which exists and will exist on this planet.'

Trust also needs to be built up for one's self; that is the best thing you can do to yourself. No matter what the circumstances are, no matter what society is saying, no matter what your own parents, spouse or son are saying, always believe in your inner voice and have faith that this voice is a reflection of your own consciousness that can never go wrong. If you have faith, your inner voice will show you the right path. You can lie to anyone, but not yourself. The truth, the absolute reality is your pure consciousness.

> ❤ *Every experience, good or bad, is to make you realize that 'trust in self' and 'others' is the foundation of a pure mind and heart.*

This realm of trust is an undisputed pillar for a fearless and liberated life. Life which is a collage of changing glorious moments; some bring happiness, some sorrows, some leave you exasperated, and some with the highest level of contemplation. This contemplation leads to self-enquiry and finally the achievement of one's own self, the Brahman, the universe, the conquering of the highest form of peace.

Gautam Buddha, the enlightened sage who was the leader and founder of Buddhism (583 BC), says,

There is nothing more dreadful than the habit of doubt. Doubt separates people. It is a poison that disintegrates friendships and breaks up pleasant relations. It is a thorn that irritates and hurts; it is a sword that kills.

Fear Nothing

Even death is not to be feared by one who has lived wisely.
—Buddha

You had nothing when you were born and will take nothing back with you when you die. Just live life with the purpose of fearing nothing and loving everything that nature has to offer. After all, there is a bit of you in everything you see around you. Our own bodies are made up of approximately seventy percent water. Ancient Indian sages believed that from water came plants, and from plants came all living creatures and the basic germ of humanity.

We are held back by fear in our everyday lives because we do not understand the simple fact that just like energy passes from one form to another, so does our soul; it is immortal. The soul isn't tied to one person forever, but only for some time, and the very basis of evolution is to be 'free'. This freedom can only be realized if our minds are free of negative thoughts and fears.

Fear is much like a false verification that appears to be real. The biggest fear for humans is the idea of losing what they have, or what they perceive in their minds as their 'own'. Fear is like fog, that can impede your vision without prior notice. Today, most human beings fear almost everything in their lives. We are scared of losing our jobs, status, power, love, money, house, property, girlfriends, youth...the list is endless. Whereas, in reality, there is nothing that you 'own' in this world; simply nothing and thus, there is no reason to fear the loss of it.

The beautiful teachings of the *Bhagavad Gita* shed light on the supreme knowledge of being fearless:

You came empty handed and will depart empty handed. There is nothing that you truly own in this world. What is yours today will belong to somebody else tomorrow, and the day after to somebody else. There is simply nothing that you are going to take with you. The pure self which is inside you, is absolutely complete, and the one who realizes the self, realizes the love of the Lord.

Fear not what is not real, never was and never will be. What is real, always was, and cannot be destroyed.

There is neither in this world nor in the world beyond, happiness for the one who fears.

These remarkable lines from the *Isha Upanishad sums* it all in just one line:

'Who sees all beings in his own self, and his own self in all beings, loses all fear.'

My biggest fear was to lose in love or rather lose my love... of being left alone one day. I thought I needed someone else to complete me and my life. Little did I know how strong I was and how complete I was in myself. But the fear was strong and insecurities kept mushrooming in the beautiful bed of passion, romance and joy.

Meeting Ram for the first time, Summer, Delhi, 1995

The ups and downs of adolescent hormones gets you to believe in this overrated concept of having a 'boyfriend', the dream 'boy', the 'prince charming'. And the choice set can be pretty bizarre from a five-foot-something, oily-haired boy to an extremely fake but rich senior who provided much needed attention and had cars which, without fail, blast out the loudest possible English music.

I was sitting on the first bench; it was the first class after assembly. A tomboyish girl approached me with a wide smile.

'Hi Kiara! Heard about you. So good to meet you. I heard you were one of the school's toppers. I am Divya. People call me Diva! It's my first day here.'

I extended my hand for a warm handshake, instantly admiring her perfect figure and sparkling confidence.

Here I am, Kiara, a class XI student of science, in a not-so-happening (in academics) Delhi school. Sweet to all, reasonably pretty, but with oddly short hair. Life had some simple agendas back then – falling in love, dancing on every possible occasion, trying to get a hot dress for my birthdays, and avoiding pimples.

It didn't take me long to scan the class and find very few familiar faces from my previous class. All my close friends had shifted to other schools and here I was, in the midst of a bunch of new faces. (Read students from rich families who didn't get admission anywhere else but here.)

One guy caught my attention for his strange looks: huge black-rimmed spectacles, a skeleton-thin body and skin that was as white as ash. It seemed as if he was waiting for me to meet his eyes, for as soon as that happened, he spontaneously gave me a beautiful smile.

I got a little uncomfortable but smiled back nonetheless. This was enough for him to strike up a conversation. He jumped up from his chair like Spiderman.

'Hi, I'm Ram, your new classmate. You know, my dad has a business related to cars. By the way, I love cars. Do you?'

What a strange way of introducing himself! I would have, under usual circumstances, dismissed him right there, but then there is something called destiny.

I'm not sure what I said in response, but we became friends from that day onwards.

January 2004

Ram came to my office once again with a pack of Ferrero Rocher chocolates. It was his way of showing his love for me, by doing these small things for me every single day. I think I had totally fallen for the idea of 'being in love'. After all, I was craving to have an 'affair', and the quest for finding my soulmate was at an all-time high.

Not just that, even the cafes at GK-I, M Block market were growing in business because of us. One of those evenings after office, I mentioned excitedly to Ram, 'You know what? I have to get this promotion, get a decent raise and then I am off to Kellogg School of Management, Chicago for another Master's in marketing.'

Ram started laughing uncontrollably, as if I had said I was going to apply for NASA's mission to Mars.

I said angrily, 'What's so funny?'

Ram replied still smiling and barely able to speak, 'Well, your mom will not allow you to even step out of your house after 9.00 p.m. and once I marry you, I will not let you stay away from me even for a day.'

'Shut up is the word for you, Ram. You see, Dad will have no problem with my going to Kellogg.'

I added quickly, 'And marriage? Are you out of your mind? Who wants to get married so early in life?'

Ram got slightly restless at that and said, 'If I had my way, I'd marry you right now.'

Suddenly our conversation was interrupted with the waiter literally banging down the coffee cups on the table. It seemed he had been having a tough day. I looked at him and said softly, 'It's all right. Don't worry, just clean up please.'

Ram suddenly held my hand and whispered, 'Listen, how about a family dinner? Mom and I can visit your place for just 'meet and greet'. You should not have problem in that at the least.'

I was extremely uncomfortable with this idea of our parents meeting each other, but couldn't say no. 'Please yaar, don't make it formal. Just a casual dinner, okay?'

Ram assured me, 'Trust me, only dinner and nothing else.'

I looked into Ram's eyes and spoke quite seriously, 'You know Ram, I am not ready for marriage yet. I need time.'

Ram got emotional, I could see that in his eyes, 'You are my life beat, Kiara. I don't understand why we need more time to get married.'

'Because you have just started your career and so have I. Also I truly feel we should give our relationship some more time,' I tried to explain

I continued talking, now with a naughty wink and smile, 'Sweetheart! I am just twenty-three and on top of that, you are my first boyfriend.'

Ram looked straight into my eyes and held my hand so tightly that it left temporary red mark on my wrist, 'Nine years of my undiluted love is not enough?'

I said softly, 'Ram, you are hurting my hand. Let go of me.'

I continued to speak while comforting my right wrist, 'It's not like that Ram. I just feel it's not right to rush into it.'

'Now not a word more, I will kidnap Mr Thakral's daughter right now,' Ram concluded as he finished his hot cup of latte.

November 2004

I was supposedly getting married the next day. I couldn't believe that the 'D' day was right here, facing me like a reality which I knew would come in my life, but not so soon. I was dead nervous, and strange thoughts were scorching my mind like a flame.

Am I doing the right thing? After all, it is marriage, not a joke. I was wondering endlessly if indeed Ram was my soul mate, the guy I always dreamed to be with, the lover with whom I'd forget everything around me. Time flies when we are together, and we share an amazingly beautiful and mind-blowingly crazy stupid love. The kind of love which is pure, unintentional, and gorgeously natural. Love which can't be explained but only *felt*.

I simply didn't want to rush into marriage. I liked Ram but certainly wasn't sure if he was my 'soul mate' and I desperately wanted more time. That feeble inner voice was constantly asking me to hold on, but *I ignored that inner voice for the first time in my life.* I felt there was something wrong but there was no rational reason for that feeling; nor could I put a finger on what was wrong. I tried telling my inner voice that I was getting married to the person who had never even thought of a girl other than me for over nine solid years. The person who patiently waited for me to say yes, the person who couldn't stay away from me even for a day. Plus, he is so amazingly handsome, and his dad treats me like his own daughter and his two younger brothers are so much fun to be with.

And, of course, with all the high intensity melodrama, finally my own parents had agreed to our match. I still remember the day when my dad first heard of Ram and how angry he was with me. He was dead against our match. He always felt that there is this 'chemistry' missing between us and I always laughed it off saying, 'Have you ever seen your chemistry with mom?'

I instantly thought of the day when Ram's parents casually came over to our house and it ended up as a formal meeting fixing up our marriage. And then somehow it was just too late for me to back out or seek more time.

Dad broke my chain of thoughts and asked me if he could talk to me for five minutes.

I gave back my signature naughty smile. 'Since when have you become so courteous to me?'

Dad said seriously in a heavy voice, 'Baby! It's something serious. I really want you to be absolutely sure about this marriage. I hope you know what you are doing. There is still time. Don't worry about anything else. I will take care of everything. But don't get married if you're not sure.'

I looked away from Dad and assured him calmly, though there was a thunderstorm in my heart. Every bit of me wanted to jump on to the offer and back out, but then I thought of

Ram, the society and everyone else. I thought of everything and everyone, except my inner voice.

'Dad! I know you are nervous, but so am I! And don't worry at all. You have seen for yourself, how deeply Ram loves me. Nothing is more important in his life than me. It was as if he was born to get married to me. Dad, I have thought about it seriously. I agree we may lack the so called 'chemistry', but c'mon, how does that matter? We will build an atrociously beautiful life and I am going to enjoy every bit of my life, no matter what. About his family's show off nature and other concerns, that is all right. Ram will stand by me in every possible situation, at least whenever I am right. And can I ever be wrong?'

I continued to speak, 'Also Dad, *sportsman nahin hua toh kya hua, handsome mechanical engineer toh hai bilkul aapki tarah!* (So what if he is not good at sports, he is a handsome mechanical engineer just like you!)

We both started laughing as I completed the sentence.

He blessed me and said softly, '*Tu bas theek rehna.*' My being fit and fine was all that mattered.

He stepped out of the room and I started looking at my mehendi covered hands and my face in the mirror which had never glowed as much before. I started thinking about our upcoming one month long honeymoon in Kerala and the last few fragments of my inner voice were muted instantly!

February 2005

We've completed three months of our marriage. I called Ram to see if he could come home early from office and also discuss if we could go out over the weekend to some remote hill station in the north, maybe Kasoli.

Ram picked up the call in one ring, 'I was about to call you.'

I said sweetly, 'Achha? Missing your new biwi?'

Ram replied angrily, 'Mom was so upset today. She just called and told me that you didn't sit with them in the morning. And why on earth do you have to speak rudely to her?'

I was flabbergasted, not expecting this at all. 'Let me explain, Ram. I got really late to office today and Mom wanted me to make lunch as well. So there was no time to sit with them for the routine chat over our morning tea. By the time I finished cooking, it was already way past ten. I skipped breakfast also because I was getting late.'

He ignored my explanation completely and continued his interrogation, 'And why did you not change your clothes when Mom asked you to?'

'Sweetheart, I just told her nicely that I am not comfortable wearing saris to office. You know I keep jumping around in the office, and there will be a free show if my saree comes undone!' And I started to laugh being my usual self.

Ram was in no mood to listen to my laughter. 'Listen, you need to understand that they have expectations. I can't have my mom crying because of you.'

I had already been upset with what was going on for the last three months, but had never voiced my thoughts to Ram or anyone else. There were amazing electric shocks for me in this new world of Ram, where everyone in the family was constantly nagging, debating, fighting over anything and everything. And how could I miss mentioning the use of abusive language, that too just for the heck of it! There should have been a statutory warning sign outside my mother-in-law's room.

'*Enter at your own risk, Madam's mood is always off.*'

I kept my calm and tried reasoning out, 'Ram, I really don't think there was any reason for her to cry over such small things. At least you should understand my intentions. I really want to keep her happy, but I can't walk, talk and wear clothes like her all the time. Last night I looked like a 'super cow' with every piece of jewellery that my neck could carry with that heavy Kanjivaram saree, and the occasion was just a casual dinner at your aunt's house. Seriously? Please Ram, I can't fight her unreasonable expectations every single moment.'

'C'mon, Kiara, Mom just wants you to change a bit. She has seen such tough times in her life and all she desires now is respect from her daughter-in-law. I love you, Kiara, but I don't want to see one more tear in my mom's eyes because of you. Do you understand?'

I couldn't understand Ram at that instant. I instantly felt like a Filmfare trophy that a Bollywood actor wants all his life and when he gets it finally, it loses its shine in the cupboard. My case was even worse.

'Are you still there?' Ram asked impatiently, 'Call up Mom now and say sorry.'

'Yes, I am here, but why do I have to say sorry when I haven't done anything wrong?'

Ram said in an authoritative tone, 'Just say sorry, and close the chapter. Don't be stubborn.'

'All right, if you insist I will say sorry to her. But Ram, this is not right...not right for our relationship in the long run. Please show some maturity in dealing with such situations. Anyway, I'll speak to you later as I have some urgent work to complete.'

Ram concluded in a happy tone, clearly ignoring what I had said about our relationship, 'See you in the evening. And tonight, my most beautiful girl in Delhi, I am not going to let you sleep even for a minute.'

With a heavy sigh I said, 'Sure! Bye.'

I wish there was a user manual on how to tackle these planted nuclear explosions in a marriage and how to keep one's sanity when everything around you is absolutely insane. Even if not a user manual, at the least the husband could have shared the potential risks for signing up to this bizzare family politics where no one gains, not even the 'chief female don' when it comes to happiness and peace.

But I did the worst thing possible, in spite of now nearly understanding the Chief – I tried being Miss Logical Funny Bone with her. The result was catastrophic and I was a complete disaster as a good Punjabi bahu.

My induction into this new world was very simple: Get drowned or learn to swim. If you can't do both, then the only option is to run – run as far as possible. I did the same, but only after a year of countless unsuccessful attempts to stay in a joint family.

●

When Nirvaan was born in 2007, it seemed nothing could ever go wrong again with my life. I was on cloud nine, and rightfully named him 'Nirvaan', which means a state of enlightenment. I had my neat epic moments, as Nirvaan was growing up fast.

Once I was on a global conference call, working from home, while my little one was quietly playing with his bright, chunky, building blocks. It was one of those difficult days when the nanny was on leave. You can do without simply anyone, but not your maid.

I was updating the India consumer marketing strategy and suddenly my little one walked up to me to tell me:

'Mamma poo...'

I signalled to him using my fingers that I needed two minutes and went back to updating hurriedly. He looked up at me to interpret this strange signal, and with absolute innocence, he increased his volume and said again, 'Mamma, poo has come.'

This time, unfortunately, he was audible enough to be caught on the global conference call. I was absolutely embarrassed to find nearly everyone on the call laughing uncontrollably. Finally, my then APAC Head, after enjoying a good laugh, said sweetly, 'Hey Kiara! It's all right. I will take it from here. You carry on.'

Unsurprisingly, I found myself smiling while helping my little one.

My life was apparently perfect from outside. I had created this illusionary world of mine which had everything – money, fame, family – but still there was something missing. Even after three years of marriage with Ram, I was still trying to find my soul mate in him, and the more I tried to rationalize, the more I got confused. I was still trying to be genuinely happy in this relationship. It's hilarious that in spite of being reasonably intelligent, I still believed in the society's time-worn advice, 'Have a child and things will be fine between you two.'

But for now, Nirvaan was everything for me. Little did I know that very soon, there would be unprecedented volcanic eruptions in my life.

March 2008

I was twenty-seven, beautiful, fit and doing very well in my professional life.

I was a working mother and was supposedly doing a good job balancing work, home and a little child. I was at the peak of my career, beauty, health and money! Could it get any better? Yes, if only my marriage was in place! As I looked up at the sky, a thought crossed my mind: marriages are made in heaven...to be executed in hell.

I smiled to myself and then thanked God from the bottom of my heart for every little thing he had given me so generously. But then I sighed; why couldn't God give me a better life partner? Somewhere deep down I knew the God particles in turn knew how to manage my life and that all I needed to do was to keep moving. I know someday I would find my soul mate in Ram...or outside of Ram.

I had known the person I married for nearly thirteen years; we were friends for nine years and married for four years. There was a time when he used to talk with respect and loved me deeply. But today he seemed to be the strangest and most incomprehensible person in my life.

A few days before the festival of Holi, Ram was watching some stupid daily soap, an irritating ritual that Ram completely loves and shares with his mom.

I think I disturbed him at the wrong time. A gaudily dressed woman in her late twenties was crying and speaking at the same time in this dramatic Hindi serial which Ram was watching with undivided attention. I think if he had his way, he would have jumped into the TV screen to wipe off her glycerin tears! The width of sindoor on her forehead could easily match the size of Bappi Da's gold chain. And she herself was wearing two fake and amazingly shoddy necklaces.

'Hey Ram, I want to visit my parents on Holi. They want to have lunch with us,' I said abruptly.

'No, we will go to my parents and then I have plans to go to Adi's house,' said Ram, without thinking even for a moment. Adi was Ram's friend from his engineering college.

I was angry and responded immediately, 'What the hell? We always end up at your parents' place on every occasion.'

He turned his face towards the TV screen. I said softly, 'Please yaar.'

Ram grunted, 'I don't want to have a vegetarian lunch on Holi. Your mom's dressing sense is atrocious and she bores me to death.'

'As if your mom is Angelina Jolie. I don't know what's going on with her fixation over red lipstick. And of course her unkindness can put the nastiest dictator to shame.'

I fought back in an aggressive tone, but also started smiling at the same time, thinking about what I had just said.

Ram obviously didn't get the humour and shouted back, 'How dare you talk about my mom like that?'

I was genuinely livid and gave back instantly, 'How dare you talk about *my* mom like that?'

'You go to your parents' place; I will go to mine.'

I concluded, 'Suits me fine... why the hell did I marry you?'

Few months had passed, not sure how many, as every day was quite similar in terms of restlessness, arguments and no conclusions whatsoever.

It was a Friday, around 12.30 a.m. and after completing daily chores, just when I was about to sleep, I received an urgent mail from a team member.

Ram asked sleepily, 'Whom are you chatting with?'

I said casually, 'No one, just replying to an urgent email. Our campaign needs to be released tomorrow. Just approving the campaign.'

Ram said crossly, 'Can't you focus on some housework as well? I don't even remember the last time you made chapatis. You know I don't like it when the maid makes them.'

'What is wrong with you, Ram? It's midnight. You know I work non-stop like a robot...taking care of my work, Nirvaan, his homework, his school pick-up, his health, your complicated Punjabi dishes, your weekend get-togethers and most importantly, the weekly torturous homage to the in-laws. And you are sulking over chapatis? Disgusting is the word for you.'

'Who is asking you to work? You are working for yourself and your freaking property. Sit at home.'

I gave a cusp reply, 'As if you are working for me and Nirvaan. I give an equal share, if not more, towards the running of this house.'

Ram was on a spree now. He consciously increased his tone, the words now coming out of his mouth seemed to have special effects.

'Ya right! I expected a 'normal' wife and not a super woman in a short skirt. You know mom doesn't like all this.'

The moment I heard 'mom doesn't like it', I boiled inside and tried my level best to not raise my voice.

I said sharply, 'Then why on earth did you marry a girl who freaking never wore a sari while you were dating her? Now even you have a problem with my clothes... Sometimes I feel I am choking with you.'

'You need to understand you are married. I guess you're simply not the kind,' Ram said rudely.

I was sardonic and responded at the speed of light. It was like a rapid fire round. I had to win, but had no clue why.

'Yes, not the kind who hails from a village in Punjab, probably who just passed her 12th class without a backbone of her own. Her only goal in life would be to make you butter chicken, and make sure you get laid every night. You should have married someone of your mom's choice.'

'Indeed! I wish I had listened to my mom before marrying you…and after that too,' Ram delivered the final blow in the highest pitch possible. It hit the stumps and I was emotionally bowled out.

I am sure the street dog, the colony security guard as well as my next door neighbour were all helplessly exposed to Ram's thunderous voice.

I responded emotionally, in a calm tone. I could barely speak now. 'You know what, you can only hurt me because I let you hurt me.'

'I have work tomorrow. Just shut up and sleep,' Ram said, completely overlooking the tears in my eyes and the pain in my heart.

That night, I nearly made up my mind to leave Ram, but something invisible, probably a simple intermolecular hydrogen atom, was asking me to hold on to the marriage, probably for Nirvaan and maybe for old times' sake when I mistook Ram's obsession with me for 'love'. I had also begun to doubt myself now.

'Where did I go wrong? Why is Ram so angry, frustrated and always ready for a fight for the last six months?'

However, there was also an internal fear; a fear of living apart from my husband; fear of what might happen. How successful would I be as a single mother? Above all, Nirvaan had done no wrong here. Why should he not get the best of both worlds and notably, both his parents?

November 2008

I visited my dad's place in Delhi on a Saturday afternoon. I had had a major fight with Ram the previous night; there were no major reasons but we were still in combat mode. I felt we were like two hostile countries trying to win a piece of land, but had no clue what to do with that land. And the more we tried snatching, the more unreasonable we were becoming.

Ana looked at my pale face and brought me a cup of coffee. It was her way of pulling me into a conversation that I would otherwise avoid like the plague.

Ana is my younger sister. Although she is my uncle's daughter, in every sense of the word, she is like my real sister.

Tall, beautifully vibrant and absolutely rock solid when it came to managing emotions, Ana's clarity of thought had always amused me while we were growing up together in our big fat joint family. I used to be her mentor for all kinds of school activities from science projects to drama scripts to debate preparations. And she in turn was my emotional support, my soundboard, my listening pal and in certain cases, my confidante.

She would be the first one to know about everything going on in my life and would always come up with simple solutions to the rare but high-octane emotional melodramas in my life.

I remember dragging her for an almost two-hour-long walk every night for nearly six months. (I wanted to be a size zero for my wedding.) She would patiently walk with me every single day and tirelessly remind me that I looked perfect and that there was no need for me to shed any weight.

During these walks, we used to endlessly discuss Ram and his passionate love for me.

'What's wrong with you? Why don't you just move on?' said Ana, while she handed me the hot coffee and I gave her a weak smile. She started off by sensing everything that was going on in my mind. She didn't even have to ask.

I said fervently, 'I am scared to do that.'

'I don't understand your fear. Get a hold of yourself. Why don't you talk to him once and for all?'

I tried explaining the situation to her. 'We don't talk dear; we are either silent or we argue. We don't even spare a topic like diapers when it comes to subjects of conflict. Yesterday, he went on and on about why Nirvaan's backside is red and that it might have something to do with the brand of diapers I buy.'

'Listen I can't bear to see you like this,' Ana said.

'Do you think he is having an affair?' I said without thinking too much. I also don't know why I said it because I trusted Ram every bit.

She smiled spontaneously, as if she was reading me, 'I don't think he can ever make this mistake again.'

'Very funny!' I said with a feeble smile.

Ana pleaded, 'Please didi! No drama. You are so successful professionally; you are young, intelligent, and cheerful and have always got on well with others. Why are you sulking over such petty issues?'

'I don't know, Ana. I am just too confused. I think Ram feels guilty about living separately from his parents. You know I just can't get along with his mom. Also, I think something is bothering him which he is obviously not sharing with me.'

'Even you are not staying with your parents. He is not a five-year-old kid. Listen you better solve this mystery and end the misery before it eats you up,' said Ana. She was visibly worried about me.

I said sadly, 'Chuck it. Let's go for a movie with all our cousins. You call them and let me sit with grandma for some time.'

August 2009, Saturday, 5.00 p.m.

I called Ram and he disconnected my call, as usual. We hadn't conversed properly for the last six months, except for nano-second conversations over Nirvaan's vaccination or health.

I called up again and within seconds he cut the call. I called the third time and asked him the two most irrelevant questions.

'Where are you? Who are you with?'

He shouted, 'Why can't you just let me be? I don't want to talk to you.'

I said angrily that I thought I needed a divorce as we couldn't be fighting like cats and dogs every single day. He in turn shouted, 'Go to hell!' and hung up on me.

I sat there feeling terrible that my childhood friend had turned into this man. When you are upset and emotional, you end up doing what you would never have done if you were calm. I called him again, but I had no idea why I was doing it and what I would say.

Ram's voice was trembling, 'If you call me one more time, I will crash my car.'

I snapped back, 'Let me die and you will be free.'

'Kiara, I will be glad if you do...'

It felt as if someone had shot me in my heart. His last words were spinning in my head. I was shivering with pain and crying profusely, tears pouring out from the deepest caves of my heart. I felt there was nothing worth living for and I simply wanted to die that very moment.

My mind's neurotransmitters graciously poured out various options; jumping out of the ninth floor apartment, consuming poison, slashing my wrists or – a novel idea – getting into a fatal accident.

As I was contemplating the best possible option with a comprehensive SWOT analysis of each option, I was startled by my BlackBerry; it was ringing at full volume. I ignored it the first time but it rang again and wiping my tears reluctantly, I spoke softly into my pearl white companion.

'Hello!'

It was Shalini, a thirty-six-year-old corporate diva, my ex-colleague, NYC returned, super-hot, and super-loving. Above all, just like an elder sister who is always there to protect me, she creepily makes an entry every time I am at my lowest.

Shalini excitedly announced, 'Hey babes. You've got to believe this. Our super stud Sandy is getting married to this girl...'

After a pause she continued excitedly, 'Her name is Basanti!'

Spontaneously, my heart took over my mind and my lips stretched within seconds. I was laughing unrestrainedly.

After a hearty laugh that lasted for almost one minute, she spoke hurriedly, 'Okay Madam, we all are catching up to take up Sandy's case. See you at Turquoise Cottage at 8.00 p.m. Love you... Be there!'

Before I could refuse or say something, she hung up.

Of course, there was no deadline to die and how could I miss making fun of Sandy with my super-funny ex-company gang over his newly acquired obsession named Basanti? I pushed the suicidal thoughts aside and promised my mind I would come back to the problem the very next day.

I had a quick shower and wore my favourite one-piece blue dress with a dab of lip gloss and kajal. I looked beautiful and I smiled back at my appearance in the mirror while giving a final look at my long, dark hair.

I looked at little Nirvaan who was fast asleep, unscathed by what was going on in his so-called super mom's mind precisely thirty minutes ago.

A tremendous storm of guilt swamped me as I looked at his innocent face. I kissed him gently and took him in my lap, told my maid to make dinner for Ram and stormed out of the house telling myself I would never ever think of such rubbish again.

Lost in deep thought and in a hurry to reach on time, I forgot to take my phone with me.

That night I reached home at eleven. Nirvaan had fallen asleep in the car. I got out of the car and just when I was about to put Nirvaan on my lap, a shadow appeared from nowhere.

I froze and suddenly turned to face the shadow. It was Ram, who was not ready for this face-off. He had been waiting for me anxiously the whole evening. Before I could speak, he hugged me tight and started to cry copiously. At that moment, he was like a child who had just realized that he had broken his favourite toy beyond repair.

'Kiara, I am really going through a tough time at work. I can be asked to leave any day and you are so busy with Nirvaan and your high profile job that I just started getting agitated about anything and everything. I have been venting the anger on you. I am also deeply disturbed about our constant fights over both in-laws and the fact that you are so successful and I am not. I love you from the bottom of my heart. I am really very sorry; I will not be a jerk, please don't ever leave me, we will sort everything out. I love you and can't live without you.'

He seemed genuinely sorry. It had been a weak moment when I had felt like ending my beautiful life and now I realized the importance of being fearless, no matter what happens. That evening certainly had its similarities with the over-dramatic Bollywood movies of India. All was well that night and from there on. It's not that all our problems got sorted miraculously; however something strange indeed happened that night. The experiences of that night had made me realize the completeness of my own character.

I got over the fear of losing Ram. I was complete in myself with or without him and that thought in itself eased my expectations from Ram. I didn't fear death and above all, I did not fear life. I wanted to live every moment and never ever looked back again. I wanted to push myself to do more in life, both at the personal and professional front. I was ready to clear away cobwebs of insecurities and fear. I was happy that I wouldn't be wasting my precious moments in sulking over any negative influences in my life; either I cut them out or repair them. Period.

I promised to make the most of my inner energy to achieve my dreams. I wouldn't accept any mediocrity when I knew I was fearless. I would cultivate my own 'cult life' and help it grow naturally and fearlessly.

●

There comes a day in each of our lives when we feel like embracing death over life. We have to understand that it's just a moment and just like no moment is ever the same, no frame of our life is the same. It is continuously changing; the sad moments will go out of the window within hours, if not within minutes.

Fear is nothing but a figment of our imagination; we fear that something might happen, not something that has happened in the past or is happening right now. You are here in the present moment but your mind is in the future scaring the daylights out of you. This is one of the reasons for all the anxieties, restlessness and corrosion in our relationships. If you fear nothing, you can achieve almost everything.

❤ *The mind is a master troublemaker; it always tries to deny the present. It wants to run away from it. The more we identify ourselves with 'moh' (attractions) and 'maya' (illusions), the more we suffer.*

The spiritual teachings of various saptarishis say:

Emotional pain is ultimately an illusion. An illusion created by the mind. Pain is unavoidable as long as you indentify it with your mind. And every pleasure and emotional high contains in itself the seeds of pain. As humans, we always want to hold on to a pleasurable situation. Instead of seeking peace and love inside, we rely on others to deliver it to us. This is a position of denial where you are constantly trying to match the frequencies of other people's minds without being fully aware of your own frequency.

I saw how easily my once beautiful relationship turned sour – from a source of happiness to that of excruciating pain. The negative attracts more of the negative, and the more you try to win this game, the more you lose.

The biggest gift you get from God is a bad time, because that teaches you in the real sense what is good in your life. When one stays in a state of tranquility in good or bad times, this is what brings him ultimate joy.

Two birds live on the same tree,
Inseparable, mutual friends
One bird eats the fruit of pleasure and pain
The other looks on without eating
The one who is detached from pain and pleasure is heading
for the supreme human destiny.

—*Rig Veda*

The biggest fear of human kind is death and this legend from the *Katha Upanishad* made me realize the beauty of death and the importance of every breath I was taking.

In the beginning of the *Katha Upanishad,* Nachiketa, a young man, has an endearing dialogue with the God of Death, Yama. He is offered all the wealth, money and other manifestations of happiness including a beautiful woman. But he politely refuses all of it, as he knows well that all this is meaningless and impermanent.

His quest for knowledge is superior enough and nothing can dissuade him from drinking the amrit of ultimate truth. Impressed by his relentless desire for supreme knowledge, Yama grants him a wish.

Nachiketa chooses to ask one of the most important questions human beings have.

Says Nachiketa to Yama: 'These pleasures last for just a while. Keep your horses and chariots to yourself, the dancing and music as well. Never can one attain happiness by wealth. I urge you to answer my question.'

When Yama agrees to answer, he asks gently, 'What happens when we die?'

Yama responds by saying, 'The ignorant run after sensory pleasures and fall into the cycle of numerous births and deaths; but the wise, knowing that the self, the soul is deathless, try to attain the lord of love within themselves and become one with him. The supreme one is beyond name, fame and form. It has no beginnings, no ends. Beyond time and space, it's immortal. Those who achieve self are forever free from death. When the body dies, the self does not die.'

The Art of Detachment

The art of detachment is the easiest path to perfect the art of living

I learned the theory of detachment through various personal experiences, both good and bad. Obsessive attachment is a state of mind where you become so attached to anything living or non-living that it prevents you from living life to the fullest.

To be fully alive, you need to be free and no matter what happens, never let go of this freedom. Before I get more sentimental about it, here is an example.

Just like you defecate in the morning and detach yourself from your own creation, don't forget to detach yourself from all the negatives (read shit) in your mind before you hit your bed.

One of the best ways to become detached is to forgive and forget.

Forgive anyone who has caused you pain, resentment, and discomfort. You never know if you or the person will even be alive the next day. Why do you want to carry this burden and live in the past forever?

Forget anyone or anything that has given you extreme happiness, if the person or the situation doesn't exist in the 'now'.

Similarly, it doesn't make any sense to sulk over the fact that the person or the situation is not present in the now anymore. Instead, remember the good times and just move on. Detach yourself graciously and live in the present moments of glory.

> *By letting it go, it all gets done. The world is won by those who let it go. But when you try and try, the world is beyond the winning.*

> —Lao-Tzu
> (Chinese philosopher, founder of Taoism)

Gurgaon, May 2012

Heena is my vivacious, divorced, super cheerful friend. Her favourite pastime is to pose for photographs to upload on Facebook. A VP (the title matters to her) in a real-estate firm, she is amazingly insecure and madly in love or rather in pain, with a celebrity anchor for the past three years. Her only goal in life is to get married ASAP to this 'dude' who thinks he is the biggest gift to women kind.

I was extremely tied up for the last few months with the biggest smart phone launch in Asia; my work required to me to travel to Singapore which was my second home by now. I knew Heena was not doing very well in her current relationship and the endless sessions from all her well-wishers telling her to 'just move on' had not helped her. She was just getting more and more engrossed in the relationship and getting hurt in the process.

That night I called her twice, but my calls went unanswered. Heena usually called back within seconds.

That had gotten me worried already. Later, at around three in the morning, my BlackBerry beeped. I reluctantly picked it up to see Heena's SMS:

Keep smiling Kiara. Take care. God bless.

For a second my heart sank. Why the hell was she sending me a message this late? I called her and her mobile was switched off. I tried calling her mother, but it went unanswered again. I couldn't sleep and knowing what your mind can do to you when you are low, I flung myself out of bed.

Nirvaan and Ram were fast asleep and there was no point in disturbing them. I jumped into my car and left for her house in Faridabad which was a decent one hour drive from Gurgaon.

By a quarter past four, I was ringing her bell crazily. It seemed the bell would fall off if I had rang it one more time. The street dogs gave me a look as if to say that these humans can't even stop with their drama at night. I looked apologetically towards them and started ringing the bell again.

She opened the door finally and there she was, a total wreck. I had not seen her for the last three months. Her beautiful face looked like that of the actress in *The Exorcist*. For a minute I was scared.

I hoped I was not looking at her ghost. Her eyes were swollen; she must have put on at least five kgs; her cheeks had a couple of red, full-blown pimples and her skin was pale yellow.

'Why are you dressed up for Halloween in July?' I said.

She was crying and speaking at the same time, 'Shut up Kiara. Rajat left me. I am such a loser. He refused to marry me. Imagine, three years and he made a fool out of me.'

'So?' I said quite casually.

'Are you mad, Kiara? What do you mean?'

'Because I know how you are feeling,' I gave her a tight hug.

She showed me messages he had sent her,

Good for nothing used up shit!

I rarely lose my temper, but when I do, I become a dynamite.

At 4.45 a.m., I dialled Rajat's number. I kept calling repeatedly till he finally answered.

'Who the hell is it?'

'This is Kiara, Heena's friend...' and then I was on a spree.

'I called up to tell you that you are a duck-head, super-duper loser! Not because you dumped my friend, but because you are not kind. You could have at least been polite while letting her go. Don't forget, life comes around to a full circle... It's absolutely your choice to be in a relationship or not and I respect that, but you have no right to demean her and call her names. Don't ever call her again. And one more message on any freaking messaging platform on the planet, I am going to turn you into CH_3CH_2OH and put it in my martini with a dash of lemon! Then you are going to be flushed out of a public toilet. I guarantee that! Good bye!'

Within a few minutes, she got a message:

I am sorry Heena. I am really sorry. Let's talk.

Heena replied: *It's all over. Thanks for everything.*

Heena then began laughing like a little kid whose deep wounds had been miraculously healed. Amused and detached.

She chirped, 'CH_3CH_2OH is methanol? No, no it's ethanol. Oh I know! It's ethyl alcohol...'

'Stupid! Ethyl alcohol and ethanol is the same,' I could barely say as I was laughing so hard.

Heena gave a peaceful sigh and her signature smile, 'Crap it! Who cares? Thank you, Kiara.'

'That's what friends are for! You should spend your life with someone who makes you feel like somebody instead of nobody. Rajat is simply not the man for you.'

She made some masala chai for us and soon I left her house feeling happy and content.

The morning sun rays fell on my car and coincidently the radio played the song *It's my Life*...I instantly remembered Lord Vishnu who had taught the demon Mahisasura a lesson in one of the legends I had heard from my grandmother. And I instinctively smiled, thinking of Rajat as a demon.

The demon Mahisasura destroyed by the Hindu supreme lords. Ancient sculptures at Mahabalipuram, Tamil Nadu, India

If you are looking for love, the best chance of finding it is to go with the flow, take hints from the universe (the Brahman), have peace within and simply be receptive to the abundance of opportunities that God presents to you. And if you are lucky to find your soulmate, just don't let him or her go because of any external circumstances and societal pressures. True love is the most precious gift a human can get in his lifetime. *Kamasutra*, the most profound ancient Indian scripture on sex and love, explains the importance of 'love' in a simple yet extremely powerful manner. There is a verse in Kamasutra that says:

There are different means of gaining happiness in this illusionary world, most astonishing being wealth, power and love. A wise man, if he has to choose one, would only chose 'love'. True love is like a cosmic alignment of one's body, heart and mind, all dancing to the same eternal tune of happiness and contentment.

❤ *Be like a bird; keep flying high. And never get attached to a tree so much that it clings to your own existence...the bird's real purpose is to fly... fly high!*

The enlightened being, though functioning in this world and doing all his/ her daily chores and what is required, does nothing, for he seeks nothing. Remain pure at heart, but from the outside, engage in the appropriate actions of this materialistic world. He who is friendly even to the one who is about to murder him, he who is loving even to the lover who has cheated him, he who is kind even to the person who has robbed him of all wealth and power, *is a seer of truth*. He who is free from ego, and who is utterly non attached to anything here on this planet, is liberated, is free, is a soul that can go beyond birth and death. Imagine loving everything around you yet being unattached – this realm is a beautiful way of experiencing life's every moment.

If you are afraid that you will not get what you want or you are afraid of losing what you have, then you have attachments. To get rid of these attachments, free yourself into a state of appreciation and gratitude towards what you have now. The fear, the strings of negativity, will be out of your mind in a few moments.

One can still understand attachments in relationships, but being attached to any physical possessions like property, cars, jewels and money is absolutely foolish. The day you know and realize that each of these material possessions are with you only for some time, that is the day you will realize the power of detachment to achieve boundless happiness.

Time doesn't wait for anyone. Be the master of your time and don't waste even a single moment on irrelevant attachments in your life. Life is the most beautiful gift given by God; live it to the fullest and be absolutely free.

Believe me, the sensation of being free is the most liberating essence of 'life management'. Keep your life simple and detached. Find the higher purpose of your life which is spiritual advancement rather than mere material advancement such as in the case of money, career and possessions. There is simply nothing that you will take away from this life except your soul which never dies. Cultivate a child-like passion; explore new things in life; experience the moments that are so unique to your own life; and above all, elevate yourself towards the higher consciousness of love, kindness and serenity.

I am deeply inspired by Mahatma Gandhi's view on detachment. He said that the man who observes self-control in thought, word and deed, right in the midst of the world, is verily the true ascetic. If things do not bind us and if we are not attached to things even when they are easily available to us, that is the greatest test of our detachment rather than merely withdrawing to a lonely forest.

He who would be serene and pure needs but one thing, detachment.

– Meister Eckhart
(1260-1326, German mystic)

Kindness is Your Character; Don't Lose It

Kindness in words creates confidence. Kindness in thinking creates profoundness.
Kindness in giving creates love.

—Rao-Tizer (4ᵗʰ century BC)

Being kind in action, speech and thought says a lot about one's character. Evil is nothing but an absence of kindness. An act of kindness can touch your heart and soul in a manner that cannot be described in mere words. Kindness has a phenomenal positive impact not only on yourself, while performing the acts of kindness, but also on the wellbeing of the entire society. Not a single act of kindness goes wasted in this universe. It is like a seed that has all the making of a forest full of fruits and flowers; an incredible value that can only grow with time. A kind person is always full of positive energy, joy, and peace that are ever-lasting. It is so beautifully natural that it can leave him or her in a heaven of contentment.

Says Saint Kabir Das (a mystical poet and great saint of India, born in the year 1440):

दयाभाव हृदय नहीं, ज्ञान थके बेहद।
ते नर नरक ही जायेंगे, सुनी साखी शब्द।।

Daya bhaav hridaya nahi, gyaan thake behad
Te nar narak he jayenge, suni suni saakhi shabd.

They have no mercy in their hearts. They are tired because of the labor of gaining knowledge. They will definitely go to hell as they know nothing but dry words.

Such powerful words of wisdom from an ancient poet who seems to have foreseen that the ever-developing human society would one day fare miserably as far as kindness was concerned. We have come to a juncture where we are living merely for food, shelter, money and sex, forgetting our human traits which are to love, respect and be kind to one and all.

Kindness in every possible form of action, will, speech and thoughts is necessary to our existence; so much so that Goethe (a renowned German author and statesman) described kindness as 'the golden chain by which society is bound together'. Kindness is essential and absolutely mandatory in order for humans to evolve and coexist harmoniously.

January 2013

I landed in Mumbai. There is something unique about Mumbai beyond its crowded streets, traffic and loads of chaos. This distinctiveness comes from the local people who are warm, courteous and extremely respectful to women. The excited Maharashtrian cabbie asked me if it was the *Hyatt Regency* or the *Grand Hyatt* I wanted to go to. I gave him the right name and he gave me a look as if to say that I was in safe hands, so I could sit back and relax!

I had to meet my advertising agency for a quick catch up at noon before the biggest encounter of my life.

I hurriedly checked in and parked myself in the beauty salon in the hotel. I wanted to look drop dead gorgeous as if 'the' SK was going to leave his hottest Bollywood heroines to date me! (But that doesn't stop you from trying, does it?)

I wore my treasured purple dress, accentuated my clear skin with a dash of peach blush, applied nude lip colour with gloss and pleaded with the hair stylist to make my hair look like the best artwork possible.

'So are you auditioning for a TV show?' enquired the hair stylist.

I instantly thought why she didn't say films and said, 'No, no. Just a meeting with a Bollywood star.'

The stylist excitedly asked, 'Who?'

I said reluctantly, 'Sanbir.'

The stylist almost jumped in excitement and said, 'Really? Wow! Don't worry, ma'am! We will do cross hair pleats with iron-shine and slight curls towards the end to suit your round face.'

God knows what that meant! But she promised me that I would look great. I closed my eyes and started daydreaming about Sanbir while the stylist worked on my strands of hair one after the other.

I was about to meet the biggest youth icon in the country; the young Bollywood super star; a marvellous actor and the extremely good looking Sanbir Kapur!

I was a diehard fan of this gifted actor. We were supposed to meet in the afternoon to discuss the brand endorsement strategy and the new script for my company's television commercial.'

I, along with the four other members of the communications team reached Sanbir's house and were ushered into his living room. The place was aesthetically and painstakingly done. Every piece of furniture seemed handpicked from the glorious cinematic legacy of his family. Acting was in his genes and here he was, the biggest, the best and the hottest actor, right in front of me. He was wearing light blue jeans with a white T shirt and flaunted a red baseball cap.

There was a short round of introductions and he sweetly extended his hand for me to shake.

'Hi, I am Sanbir.'

'Of course, Sanbir. I am Kiara. I lead Brand Marketing for the Asia Pacific region. I am so glad to meet you.'

'Hey, nice to meet you too. Make yourself comfortable,' he said sweetly.

He used the intercom to ask for tea and snacks for us.

I sat on the couch next to Sanbir and started the presentation, trying to give him a glimpse of the agenda for the meeting.

As I was narrating the brand strategy and the landscape of the campaign concept, he leaned forward a little to look straight into my eyes. I almost froze for a moment. The biggest Bollywood icon was so close to my face, I could nearly hear his breathing and smell his icy-cool mint perfume. Our proximity was straight out of a romantic movie, if only I could magically delete all the side characters present in the room. I could barely fight off the strong urge to kiss him.

Sometimes, the mind does you a favour, although rarely. My mind told me, 'Madam, you are married and have a kid.

Plus, you are the brand head of a prestigious MNC. You can't kiss SK in front of five people and that too in his own den!'

I nodded and continued speaking about the 'go to market plan' and why our new product was the best thing ever after the Wright Brothers' invention.

But my drooling over him had not stopped. 'What if he slaps you in return?' my mind wondered.

I shivered at this thought, shook away the last few fragments of disarray and focused on what I was narrating.

Never mind that we never kissed except for a quick friendly hug which he did gracefully, even with quite a few men in the room. I got him on my BBM friend list and it seemed God had finally given me a priceless award of a lifetime!

I swore to God if there ever was one sin allowed, it would be for SK, with SK and only SK!

But there is something I gained from the Bollywood star which was far more superior, enriching and permanent than a mere kiss. Behind his larger than life persona, there was an enduring down-to-earth serenity. I was very impressed by his humbleness; there was no air of a celebrity about him; he was as normal as any one of us. His super stardom was overshadowed by his own sweet and kind aura.

When one of our team members came late to the meeting, he got up himself to pull up an extra chair. He also handed me a cup of tea to ensure that I was sipping the hot green beverage while I was talking non-stop. Not once did it seem that I was talking to a super star. He was just like any one of us – dedicated, listening and contributing to the value creation, and being the perfect host.

In short, he taught me the importance of being who you are and not what others expect you to be.

That very day, besides being further infatuated with Sanbir, I promised to stay calm, grounded and kind, no matter how successful I became *(if at all I ever do)*.

Later that night, memories of that hot Sunday of November 2010 came alive, when I experienced the word 'professional kindness' in a unique and unexpected way.

I was in the middle of a TVC shoot in Lavasa, when I got a frantic call from Samay, a young thirty-year-old retail marketer in the team. He sounded nervous.

He declared, 'The collaterals worth USD 25,000 that we needed to deliver to all channels have got wrong product specifications!'

I was worried. I promptly checked the final creative that had reached my inbox for approval and it all looked fine.

It meant that the advertising agency had made a mistake while sending out the artwork to the printer. And again at the printer level, my team had made a mistake by not checking the proofs. And now here we were with a monster problem!

Firstly, who was going to pay another USD 25,000 for printing the entire set of collaterals? Also, the collaterals had to reach every channel in the next three days which meant that the fresh printing had to happen that night. To add to that, Samay's team had to deliver it within one day instead of the usual three to five days.

Look at scenario 1 and scenario 2. Can you guess what happened?

Scenario 1

Samay called to inform me and had simultaneously typed an email to Jasbinder our Senior Communications Manager. The mail was copied to me, the National Sales Head and to the VP APAC Marketing.

> **Subject:** *URGENT AND IMPORTANT – Huge mistake in collaterals and hence massive channel readiness delay...*

It looked like he intended to write the whole email in the subject itself, explaining the gravity of the situation (The agony is easily comparable to a doctor revealing a diagnosis of cancer to his patient). The fact that all hell had broken loose on the launch of our latest smartphone was painstakingly communicated in the email. He meticulously used capital letters, different font colours and all possible heavy duty words like 'disaster', 'disappointed', 'grave mistake', 'unfortunate' and above all 'What a shame!'

Immediately there was a wave of panic all around. Blame games began in full swing and it seemed like a hopeless situation from every angle. The National Sales head wrote to the India CEO explaining how sales would be negatively affected due to this delay in channel readiness and that of course, the marketing team is responsible. The VP of Marketing expressed his utmost disappointment in the entire marketing team in a well-crafted email. The last line therein was trying to shout very hard: Take actions immediately!

Meanwhile, Samay sent out another email to the entire retail team about the potential delays and possible demise of the new smartphone.

The respective regional retail leads also panicked and informed the distributors about the delay; the distributors, in turn, created more panic by saying that the competition had already intensified its promotional activities and here we were without even a product brochure.

I frantically called my Communications Manager, Jasbinder, and shouted at him. He in turn shouted at the agency head, who in turn shouted at his junior creative designer who in turn shouted at his wife who had called him twice while he was being shouted at and who in turn, shouted at her little five-year-old who came to show her his drawing of a butterfly.

Finally, it took us three days to get a special budget approved by Finance, and one of the marketing campaigns was shot down to compensate for this 'collateral damage'.

The channel was completely ready only after three days of the product hitting the stores and obviously there was a loss of USD 25,000 to the marketing budgets.

I wanted to smack Samay and I also, quite grudgingly, decided to screw his appraisal. Jasbinder decided to take revenge by swearing not to do any urgent work for the retail team and he also swore to teach Samay a lesson sooner than later.

Scenario 2

After receiving the bad news from Samay, I immediately had a conference call with Jasbinder and the agency head. I communicated the problem and requested the agency's help. The advertising agency head was extremely apologetic about the situation and agreed to cover seventy-five percent of the printing cost. Meanwhile, my Communications Manager ensured that he got the corrected artwork to the printer within an hour.

I also made a separate call to Jasbinder who apologized again for the mistake and promised that it would never be repeated.

Samay meanwhile never wrote any email but instead called all the regional retail sales leads to let them know that we had a situation on our hands. He let them know that the printed merchandise was arriving a day late and hence we needed to ensure that we worked overnight, along with the distributors and circle heads, to deliver the collaterals across the length and breadth of the country.

Samay and I then called the printer and tried convincing him to give us a twenty-five percent discount on this job as it was the printer's duty to ensure the proofs were approved by the designated authority before printing.

After a solid thirty minutes of soft arguments, Samay softly said to the printer, 'Bhai, please do it. We will be grateful.'

Heaving a heavy sigh, the printing agency head said, 'Okay sir, as you say.'

Going by Samay's expression, it seemed as if the guy had just agreed to marry off his most beautiful daughter to Samay. Samay started thanking him profusely and was very close to saying, 'I am going to keep you (the printing guy) happy forever!'

Our printing job was put on the highest priority in the work order. Eventually, as a team, we met the deadline for the delivery. Miraculously, the distributors also helped with their respective fleets on the street and every shop possible had the corrected collateral a day before the launch.

Thankfully, it was the second scenario that turned into reality.

The whole team had pulled together through a crisis just like a family. No one was interested in pulling anyone down, but instead wanted to get the job done for the company and very importantly, for their colleagues as well. Even partners came to the rescue and an amazingly bad situation was turned into something to celebrate.

I came back from the shoot and met Samay. I couldn't help thanking him abundantly and he, in turn, thanked me for helping him with the channel readiness.

That day, I promised myself that I would help every single colleague of mine. Life comes full circle; if you can help your friends, family and loved ones, then why not your colleagues with whom you spend most of your day? It isn't too taxing to be genuinely nice and kind. I will always be thankful to Samay for this; to be kind and helpful to everyone.

Samay has always been the funny, flamboyant good looking go-getter and a big show-off too, for he suffers from a self-complimenting syndrome, but has a heart of gold. He is probably the best person to stay in the Sheesh Mahal of Agra. He can't stop gushing about himself, but never hesitates to helps others.

August 2012

I landed at Jakarta Airport at 10.00 p.m. It was an urgent official visit and hence I had to get my visa on arrival. It was my third time in Indonesia, but I had never hated coming to this country so much before. I was standing in this never-ending queue for my visa when my BlackBerry started to ring.

I said in a restless voice, 'Samay what's up? Calling me at this hour? I am in Jakarta. All well?'

Samay sounded extremely happy, 'Hey sorry Kiara, but I could not wait. Have you landed alright? Listen I have good news to share.'

I began to tease him as usual, ' Don't tell me, another model has agreed to go out with you.'

'Nahin yaar! Listen, I am promoted; your best friend is a Senior Manager.'

I instantly smiled back at Samay, 'You deserve it every bit, Samay. I can't tell you how happy I am for you.'

Samay was different that day and seemed modest. He chirped, 'I am still learning. A long way to go, buddy.'

'*Chal chal ab natak mat kar*. Where are you treating me and rest of the gang?' I said excitedly.

He said softly, 'You choose the place, madam.'

'Yeah let me get back and we'll party hard! And by the way, do you know why you got this promotion?'

'Yep, because I am too good for this company,' he said.

'Very funny! No, and I may sound a bit philosophical, but the truth is that you are a benchmark in professional compassion,' I submitted seriously.

'Yeah right! Okay I'll let you go, come back soon. Bye!'

I kept the phone down and started smiling. I was indeed very happy for Samay. I had seen seeds of kindness in his personality and was glad that his helpful nature was getting noticed and not merely his target achievements. The visa queue didn't annoy me as much now and I started to think of the best place for a party in Gurgaon.

•

> ♥ *In this so-called corporate jungle, there have to be people planting seeds of trust, help, team work and above all, kindness. And that can only happen when you are not inhibited by mindless insecurities.*

Many friends, relatives, colleagues, bosses, partners and even customers will get immense pleasure by putting you down, at times just to gain some extra brownie points with the boss. But you have to grow out of that weakness and never lose your mind or values over such 'barmy heads'.

However, do remember that negativity breeds more negativity, so in this corporate jungle, if you sow the seeds of Babul trees, you can never get sweet mangoes. If you are kind to a person, then it is most likely that the person will reciprocate with the same kindness. Kindness is like a good virus that is so beautifully infectious that it can pass its soothing effects from one person to another in a flash.

Being kind is the most important characteristic of a strong human being. A person can never be truly rich with just money, property and jewels; he will be truly rich if his heart is full of compassion. The strength of human kindness is superbly demonstrated by Gautam Buddha in his teachings. He says,

> '*When words are both true and kind, they can change the world.*'

There is an ancient Buddhist story in the *Samyutta Nikaya,* a Buddhist scripture, which is the third of the five *nikayas* in the *Sutta Pitaka*. For me, this story demonstrates how the beauty of kindness transcends all evil and violence. The heartwarming philosophy in this legend is exceptionally relevant in today's world with its prevalence of mindless insecurities, hatred and negligible kindness.

Once there lived a demon who had a peculiar diet: he fed on the anger of others. And as his feeding ground was the human race, there was no lack of food for him. He found it quite easy to provoke anger, hatred or violence among the greedy humans. Even igniting a war was unbelievably easy for him. And whenever he succeeded in causing a big war, he would feed himself conveniently for a long time. Hatred among the humans multiplied even amongst otherwise friendly people. So for the demon, food was in abundance and at times he would even try not to overeat.

One day he thought of going to the world of gods for food; the world of gods had plenty of pleasures and negligible pains. They hardly fought or quarreled over petty issues. He went to a particular heaven whose king was Sakka, the lord of gods. He reached the place and found that Sakka was absent in the hall of the gods. He then went and sat on Sakka's throne waiting quietly for things to begin happening. As soon as the other gods saw a demon sitting on the throne and grinning, they started shouting and cursing at him. While the gods were growing more and more angry, the demon was growing more and more in strength. He was delighted that he could even feed himself in the world of gods. This is when Sakka, the divine king entered the hall and said kindly to the demon,

'Welcome, my friend! Please stay seated. May I offer you something to drink?'

As Sakka's kind words increased, the demon's powers diminished and in no time the demon shrank to a very small size and finally disappeared.

This legend touched me to the core; I myself have faced numerous personal and professional challenges and I have managed to overcome them and have emerged unscathed by using my biggest power; the power that you can't see with your naked eyes; power which is intangible yet the most valuable asset to human nature; this is the power of kindness and compassion. Try it yourself by being kind to someone who is at the peak of his or her anger and hatred towards you. Their anger will dissipate, their hatred will turn into respect and their conscience will tell them to let go of the situation.

The fact that we as human beings are capable of kind acts which have no clear material benefit for ourselves means that we can try to create lives which have meaning beyond simply survival. We are an evolved species, both morally and spiritually, and are capable of rising above purely selfish desires. Kindness defines us; it's the fundamental building block of our nature and sets us apart from all other life forms on earth. It separates the nature of human beings from that of a pack of dogs. I remember a friend who frustrated us at every party with one of his favourite dialogues that he delivered with utmost emotion and passion.

'My friends! We are no different from dogs; they run for food, shelter and sex on four legs and we run on four wheels. Sometimes, we are even worse than dogs; they at least enjoy the running. We have no purpose and no real joy; we just run and run endlessly. We need to grow in higher consciousness and not merely chase money and cars.'

He had apparently gone for an art of living course in the Himalayas for three months. He came back looking as fresh as mint and almost ten years younger. Of course, he also came back with his favourite dialogue etched in his heart and mind.

Never Stop Thanking!

The biggest contribution you can make to someone's life is to make him or her feel truly elated, and there can't be a better way than to 'thank' the person.

'Thank you' is one of the most important phrases in an individual's vocabulary. It can have a remarkable effect on your spirit; it will not matter if you are saying it or receiving it.

There is always, always, always something to be thankful for. Even if you have nothing, simply nothing, you shouldn't forget that you still have the sun's warm light and that you are alive to feel it!

What if there was a solution to all the crazy stress we face every single day? The solution is very simple – it involves nothing but simply being thankful for the good things in your life and feeling grateful for what you possess instead of sulking about what you don't have.

Various medical studies across the globe have shown that people who regularly practice feeling thankful are much happier, healthier and are also stress free. Leading researchers in this growing field termed 'positive psychology' have found that those who adopt an 'attitude of gratitude' as a permanent state of mind, experience many health benefits including better immunity and improved mental alertness.

Singapore 2012

Singapore is like a triple sundae: a beautiful cosmopolitan city of different cultures, communities and absolutely stunning infrastructure. Singapore became my second home while I was deeply immersed in my new regional APAC assignment.

On a warm and sunny Saturday in September, I visited Universal Studios – a meticulously-built theme park with amazing attractions especially designed for kids.

Nirvaan was at his naughty best as we spent time eating at various eateries, watching musical shows and trying a few crazy roller coaster rides.

I questioned the logic of literally putting your stomach in your mouth on these precarious roller coasters, but people seemed to enjoy that. People were shouting non-stop; some out of fear, a few out of excitement and others just for the heck of it. I was sitting outside a small ice-cream shack just next to the entrance to the roller coaster ride on a dark, wooden bench with Nirvaan, having some hot coffee with blueberry muffins. Nirvaan was feasting on his yogurt cone with warm carrot cake. He asked me sweetly if he could get more chocolate chip toppings for his yoghurt and I nodded. I saw him going inside the shack, proudly carrying five SGD in his little hand.

I turned to look at the roller coaster again. I saw an overweight Chinese woman pleading for the machine to be stopped. Her husband, most likely, was having the time of his life, and didn't seem to notice his distressed wife. He was noticeably happy that his wife was all cuddled up to him.

I suddenly realized Nirvaan was not back yet. I looked towards the shack but couldn't see him. For a second, my heart stopped. I looked around frantically to see if he was somewhere around it, but couldn't see Nirvaan anywhere.

I hurriedly started running about and shouting his name. I was barely able to shout and it seemed my voice disappeared into the seething mass of people.

I started asking every possible person if they had seen a little Indian boy...five years old in a blue Doraemon T shirt and grey shorts.

I was sweating, my lips were dry and tears were pouring out of my eyes. My mind was racing, trying to think of all the places he could be. I ran towards the help desk and pleaded with them for announcements. Ten minutes had passed looking for Nirvaan, but seemed as long as ten years.

During the search, I had spotted a 5D simulator. I peeped inside to find a few Malaysian girls in bright pink hijabs, eight to twelve years old. My eyes scanned each one of them, every possible game zone and all the eateries in the vicinity. Universal Studios is built on acres and acres of land; it was impossible for me to look for him in every nook and cranny. There was also the huge possibility that Nirvaan had panicked and run off in the opposite direction.

I started praying hard. Inadvertently, I was chanting the Gayatri mantra and shouting Nirvaan's name at the same time.

The announcements were in full swing. By now, the theme park crew as well as the guards had joined the search. I felt that everyone was like a member of my own family and were desperately trying to help me with an intensity that almost matched mine.

Thirty minutes passed. Then, just next to the famous Lion fountain five hundred meters away, I saw a Muslim woman in a blue hijab, with a five year old boy in her lap, trying to pacify him with some toy. I started running in her direction with my high-heeled boots in my hand.

When I was barely a hundred metres away, I realized it was Nirvaan. I started shouting Nirvaan's name at the top of my voice and within seconds Nirvaan saw me too. He freed himself from the Muslim lady and started to run towards me. It seemed like a typical Bollywood movie climax.

I threw my shoes and purse on the floor and took Nirvaan into my arms. Both of us began to sob.

I finally asked Nirvaan where he had gone. He had come out of the other end of the shack by accident; he had then started running in all directions trying to find me.

The Muslim woman in whose lap he had been sitting was standing close to me now, and said lovingly, 'He is alright. Don't worry.'

Nirvaan had been with her all this while and she had taken good care of him, buying him hot French fries with iced tea, and getting him a toy monkey to make him feel a little better while her ten-year-old son went to inform the authorities.

I must have thanked her a million times and she was a little embarrassed with my over the top behaviour. She kept saying, 'It's absolutely all right, darling...'

She was originally from the Swat Valley in Pakistan and on a holiday. Swat Valley, once a beautiful paradise on earth, was now affected by unrest and fighting.

I thanked her one more time, bidding a warm adieu and she gently said to me in a dialect which was a mix of Urdu and Hindi, '*Yeh toh Allah ki marzi hai jo usne muhje bhej diya.Ya Allah bahut kuhbsoorat hai apka shehzada.*'

When she said that it was God's will to send her for my son, who she found very beautiful, I understood that someone always watches over us.

When God created this world, I am sure he never thought that his most intelligent life forms would divide it into segments based on caste, creed, colour, religion, names, nationalities, districts, designations and the like.

That day, a respectful Muslim lady helped my child as a mother...but as a human being first. She never asked my son for his name, his nationality or his religion. She just showered him with selfless love and empathy.

I did my bit of thanking one person in my life on that action packed super dramatic day. I called my mom and after narrating all about the experiences of the day, I suddenly said to her, 'Thank you, Mom, for all that you have done for me. I really love you.'

My mom is a native of Gujarat. She was amazingly beautiful in her youthful days. No wonder my dad fell for her at first sight. But life has been tough to her since raising a son with Down's syndrome has not been easy.

Mom replied in a heavy tearful voice, 'Are you mad? I haven't done anything for you. You have always been so independent. I don't even remember if you ever asked me for anything. You are the reason for my smiles.'

Sometimes I hate my sense of humour, because right in the middle of that emotional moment, I chirped barely controlling my laughter, 'Mom, please don't speak in English. Your Gujarati accent is making me laugh.'

'I don't understand why I even picked up your call at this hour,' snapped Mom, trying to show that she was angry with me.

I said sweetly hoping to make her smile, 'Achaa, sorry! By the way, I am thankful for one more thing.'

She asked excitedly, *'Kya?'*

I was laughing and talking at the same time. 'You didn't throw a fit to marry me off to a *Gujju* boy. Imagine how terrible my life would have been.'

She was in no mood to give up. She said sharply. 'As if it's any good with a Punjabi boy.'

I laughed louder, 'You know well how to hit me below the belt. Thank you for being so kind to me.'

Mom got emotional and said sweetly, 'I hope you get all the happiness, baby! I may not say this to you very often but I really love you.'

I replied instantly. 'Please, if you love me so much, then promise me, you won't make me eat like a cow the next time I am home.'

My mom concluded sweetly, 'Will see about that. *Bas tu theek rehna.*'

> ❤ *The biggest religion on this planet is love.*

Love is the purest form of feeling human kind can experience. Love is what you need to give, to experience, to inhale, to soak and to practice unconditionally. Love is the biggest gift you can get and be thankful for. Trust me, there are very few people on this planet who can truly give and receive your love, unconditionally and unabashedly.

I think every person on this planet is the same, whether he is poor or rich; it does not matter where he comes from. At the end of the day, he is made of the same basic building blocks of life that I am made of. Biochemistry tells us that human beings are composed of different types of large molecules: proteins, nucleic acids, lipids, and carbohydrates. These molecules are held together by intermolecular forces. Imagine what would happen if all of these molecules start to fight with each other? I wonder if our body would hold out even for a day. Similarly, we human beings are held together by a spiritual force: the force of love, compassion and light. How can we survive together if we don't appreciate the very being next to us?

Beyond all the man-made mindless segmentations, I feel the lord of love is shining bright in each one of the 'kind' people.

The very foundation of kindness is to consider every single person equal; try loving and thanking each person around you selflessly. And in return, enjoy the pleasures of higher wisdom, and most importantly, the unprecedented levels of peace and joy it will bring you.

There is someone who has built the road on which you drive; there is someone who delivers milk to your house; there is someone who ensures your house gets electricity; there is someone who built the hospitals around you; there is someone who made the air conditioners that keep you cool – and we must be thankful for it all.

Thank your parents; they do the most thankless job of taking care of you at every little step.

Thank your friends for making your life so beautiful; imagine a day in school, college or at the local park without your friends around you.

Thank your colleagues for helping you to be comfortable at work.

Thank your kids for helping you become a much better person than you ever were. Thank your kids for making you go through all the forgotten school lessons all over again. (Okay, you can skip this one if you like.)

Thank your spouse for tolerating a creature like you; and you have no idea what you would get in return. (No, no, not hot sex but an abundance of warmth and reverence.)

The moment you start appreciating everyone around you, you will automatically be rewarded by appreciation. Believe me, this high is much better than any dope on this planet.

There are hundreds and thousands of people who are helping you to live your life comfortably. Thank everyone around you graciously. Thank God, and lastly, thank yourself for being a great person (only if you are!).

DA, DA and DA

Master your thoughts. Give. Be compassionate.
— Brihadaranyaka Upanishad

On one occasion, the gods and the demons approached Prajapati, the supreme creator.

Having observed great austerity, the gods went to the creator himself, and said, 'Give us wisdom.'

Prajapati answered with one word, *'DA.'*

'Have you understood what it means?' he asked.

'Yes!' they said. 'It means *Damyatta* (self control).'

'Good, then follow my instructions,' said Prajapati

Having also observed great austerity, the human beings went to the Creator and said, 'Give us wisdom.'

Prajapati answered with one word, *'DA.'*

'Have you understood my word?' he asked.

'Yes!' they said. 'It means *Datta* (to give).'

'Good, then follow my instructions.'

Having observed great austerity as well, the demons then went to the Creator and said, 'Give us Wisdom.'

Prajapati answered with one word, *'Da.'*

'Have you understood?' he asked.

'Yes!' they said. 'It means *Dayadhavam (to be compassionate)*.'

'Good, then follow my instructions.'

Out of all the Upanishads that I have read, this particular chapter of the *Brihadaranyaka Upanishad* blew me away completely. It is indeed my favourite section and no matter how many times I read it, I still feel compelled to go back to it. Every time I read it, I find newer jewels of wisdom; the knowledge gained each time is simply magnificent, glorious and insightful. It beautifully summarizes the art of living in the simplest form.

With just one word 'Da', it gives you the higher knowledge of living.

'Damyatta' – It means mastering your thoughts, your mind in the midst of any pleasure or pain. It is unbelievably relevant in today's mindless competitive world.

'Datta' – Human beings are greedy. They want to grab everything; from money to property to love. It explains the beauty of charity; not just about material giving but also charity in character, in understanding and in sacred feelings for others.

'Dayadhavam' means being compassionate, kind and merciful. The human race is becoming the Asura race defined in the ancient scriptures. Even in our daily lives, we have forgotten the beauty of kindness. We want to be cool, dressed in the best branded clothes, wearing the best perfume in the world, showing off our well-crafted shoes and using the most expensive body cleansers. But how many of us look deep down in our hearts to cleanse our internal impurities? We lie, we deceive, we turn a blind eye to someone's suffering under the pretext of living our life to the fullest and who cares a f**k about the world around? 'It's not my job; my life is already too stressful,' and things like 'If others are not doing something, why the hell should I?'

I truly believe that God is within you, the divinity is within yourself, and every possible description of diversities in the form of gods, demi gods, human, animals, plants, demons, etc., are the cycles of evolution to achieve the ultimate 'Lord of love', the state of pure consciousness which is away from any diversity, untouched by any adversity, full of peace and the ultimate reality.

The supreme yoga is the self effort. Self effort in being kind, truthful, compassionate, unconditional, unattached and mastering one's thoughts. Proximity to selfless and divine people is a boon in this Kalayuga.

> ♥ *Try to create a world around you where you hand-pick people whom you truly want to be with, who are truly having a positive impact in your life...not just in terms of money, sex or society pleasures, but in making you a nicer person with each passing day.*

The Light Within You

There are two ways of spreading light; to be the candle or the mirror that reflects it.

– Edith Wharton

The very fact that you can dream, and desire to achieve that dream is a reflection of your capacity to achieve it. According to Vedanta, each human being has a certain amount of higher consciousness and a supreme energy that can get him anything material or spiritual in his life. This energy should be ideally used for spiritual advancement and in attempting to become a better human being with each passing day. The real success is within, deep inside, in the lotus of your heart. The moment you fix a goal or a purpose in your mind, you have already realized the path for achieving it. It is like kindling an otherwise dormant fire that can sweep you away to higher levels of peace, joy and serenity. Trust yourself, be the architect of your own life and do what you absolutely love doing with utmost concentration; live every moment of this beautiful journey called life. Laugh, cry, celebrate and remind yourself every day of this amazing light within you, the brilliance of which can throw off any iota of negativity and self-doubt. This light is your power; the absolute reality that reminds you relentlessly that nothing else matters but your own higher consciousness. You are not what others want you to be, but what you feel you want to be. The last thing you can do to yourself is not to catch the signals of your inner glow.

> ♥ *The light within you is the aura which is peaceful, untouched by sin, serene and truly yours.*

The way darkness doesn't exist in the presence of light, similarly, ignorance can't exist for someone who is engaged in self inquiry.

All desires are achievable, it's up to you to how far you want to pursue the desire. The ultimate desire for human kind is to achieve inner peace; complete cessation of all desires.

Chicago, 2011

Chilly winds brushed my delighted face. I felt a warm rush of emotions as I started to walk towards the convocation hall of one of the best business schools in the world, the Kellogg School of Management. This had been my dream since the year 2001 when I first fell in love with the subject of brand marketing – to study in the world's best school for marketing.

My quest to learn the higher levels of marketing in the best school had turned into reality and I felt tears rolling down my cheeks. These were happy tears coming from the deepest caves of my heart.

As I passed the campus lake, I saw black ducks swimming in the lake. I soaked up every passing moment and occasionally wiped my tears. Nirvaan asked me if I was all right and I said, 'I couldn't be better!'

Besides the solid concepts, frameworks and business acumen, I learned something truly special: the power of human connections in creating something spectacular and the power of having people believe in it. The human connections which are beyond one's shallow identification with culture, religion, countries or colour. It is a diversified bond that you forge; something which you can't name but can truly feel.

Wednesday, 2.00 a.m.
Discussion room 'Niagra' on the second floor, James Allen Centre

The 'I' team was busy working on the hottest submission of the season. We were working hard on the live business simulation game. Our voices were soft but firm as we were locking decisions for the final round (level 9). We had been the underdogs among eight teams in total and had slowly grown, step by step. At level six, we became the closest challengers to the 'A' team, who were leaders in profit as well as market share.

The 'I' team had Benrico from Italy, Rody from Sweden, Saria from Chile, Gab from Russia and me.

'I think we should take the current product out of the market completely and re-launch it with revised specifications, and then we go full throttle after the prosumers,' I said quite seriously as if it was the matter of life and death.

Benrico disagreed, 'I think that is absolutely foolish. We are in the last round and we can't take such a huge risk. What if the segment rejects the new product.'

Gab chirped, 'I know Benrico hates rejection. And a blonde rejection can get him crazy.'

Benrico was in no mood for jokes, 'Shut up, Gab. Let's just go bizzare with the current product, increase the advertising budgets along with sales, and have a clean sweep.'

I gave my reasoning, 'Listen guys, we've got to think differently here, something which the others in the game can't think of easily. We have to get ahead of the 'A' team, not just in market shares but also profits. And the only way to beat them hands down on both fronts is to bring few strings together like an improved new product, with exact specifications which targeted prosumers want at a price which is slightly lower than the competition but such that it doesn't hit our profits due to the incremental volumes. I can get to the miracle pricing and our Saria will nail the bull's eye with product specifications.'

Rody added, 'Well I agree with Kiara, there is no point increasing the marketing and sales budgets for incremental sell through, because that won't increase market share as per my predictive brand's 'purchase intent' analysis for the current product mix.'

'You owe me, babe, on this one. I want to win this game, and this is a gorgeous risk,' said Benrico impatiently.

'Dude, trust me, we will rock the Kellogg building tomorrow morning!' I said super excitedly.

'Then lock it, sweet cup. And if we win, you have no clue, babe, how I am going to treat the 'I' team!' said Benrico with a twinkle in his eyes and a luminous glow on his handsome features.

Benrico and I initially had mild conflicts over decisions in the simulation game, especially about consumer strategy and research. But as we progressed in the game he said, 'There can be only one leader in the team, so let's go with Ms CEO.'

He would leave the final decisions to me and would say, 'Don't worry, I trust you. I trust your gut feeling; just lock it.'

Berinco was this super good looking and super intelligent multi-millionaire from Italy; he had a heart of gold and was an innovation machine. Amazingly well read, he had lofty dreams to become the next big thing after the inventor of Facebook.

Rody Zwaire owned a brand consultancy and I swear I haven't met anyone as thorough in brand marketing as he was. He was like an experienced big brother on the team.

Saria was very good in analytics and our products created in the simulator vis a vis the target audience hit the bull's eye, thanks to Saria's incredible analytical inputs. I remember telling her that she was god-gifted and she would smile brightly saying, 'Babe, you don't know all the things that I am gifted with; ask my BF!'

Gab from Russia was a very funny man and kept high stress levels at bay. He would give inputs specifically on market planning and then would simply get back to cracking jokes.

On the final day of the simulation game, the 'I' team had clocked in the highest profits in the business simulation game especially given the circumstances of the team when the game had begun. The team was given a prize that is treasured in my heart forever. I heard the marketing professor say, 'In the long history of business simulations at this college, the 'I' team has certainly created a benchmark for others to aspire to.'

Later that evening, the 'I' team and a few more friends from the class went pub hopping and by the time we reached the fourth pub, the whole group had already crossed the limit of craziness. Though I was not drunk at all, I climbed atop the bar table along with Saria and was smiling, dancing and jumping, all at the same time like an innocent little toddler. A hot French guy who had been watching me for a while asked me my name and I proudly replied, 'Well, you can call me Baby!'

I heard my 'I' team shouting, *'Baby! Baby! Baby!'* and I joined the chorus happily!

Somewhere deep down, I feel that our 'I' team would come together again at some point in the future to create something spectacular. I knew that we were friends for life and I would be grateful to this college for giving me the opportunity to make friends with such beautiful people!

●

November 2012, Saturday, 3.00 a.m.
Los Angeles

I landed in LA for an official meeting. I had high fever, a cold and severe body ache. I checked into the hotel and could barely walk to the room. I was cursing myself for taking the trip with no idea whatsoever about how the trip was going to change my life forever!

The Los Angeles weather seemed to be an amalgam of rain and sunshine. Between the occasional rainy days, the sky was a clear blue. The layers of marine clouds, which are known as June Gloom, can be seen in the sky giving you a glimpse of a spectacular sight, making most mornings overcast until noon.

I could see people in vibrant, colourful clothes on the street. Each one of them dressed in their distinctive style: LA is the centre of the US fashion and clothing industry and I found LA fashion casual, authentic and individualistic.

Sunday, 4.00 p.m.

Going to the beach is one of the most popular activities in LA, and with over seventy miles of beaches, you can find one to suit your taste; from sandy, calm, crowded beaches to remote, scenic, rocky beaches. I chose the most secluded spot on the beach, as if the whole ocean in front of me had been created just for my appreciative attention.

I was neck-deep in my thoughts about what was next in life, when I was suddenly disturbed by the feeble sound of 'Om'. I thought God had just appeared to bless me. (No, No, I wasn't that lucky!)

I looked back and saw a group of twenty-five to thirty-year olds in bright orange kurtas and jeans, hurriedly rolling out mattresses on the beach and chanting the word. I looked at them and waved a friendly hello and they gestured to me to join them. Having no reasons to say no, I readily agreed.

I started to enjoy one of the most peaceful and melodious sounds of the universe: the sound of 'Om'.

We were sitting on the sand in the Pranayam position of yoga, chanting loudly every time the waves kissed the shore.

It is difficult to describe in words what an electrifying ambience it was. It seemed the ocean was in perfect harmony with us and the water from the high tide was dancing to the tunes of eternity.

I felt as light as a feather, floating peacefully high in the sky, never to come back to any chaos on this Mrityulok. Later that evening, I met a few of my newly-made friends from the beach for dinner. I was astonished at the extent of their knowledge of Vedanta, the teachings of ancient Indian sages, the power of yoga, and above all, the amazing Upanishads. I was a little embarrassed to learn about my country's timeless wisdom from people who were distinctly non-connected with our culture and practicing it thousands of miles away from India.

One of them mentioned an ashram in an ancient town in South India called Tiruvannamalai which the group often visited.

We started ordering food and I was quite amazed to see that the whole group ordered vegetarian food. For the first time, indeed, I was not the odd one out.

'How are all of you vegetarians?' I asked.

A twenty-eight-year-old Indian girl who was a painter as well as an economics professor readily replied, 'Why do we need to add the flesh of an innocent animal to our bodies when we can easily do without it?'

Over delicious continental food, we started talking about the Gayatri mantra, the most powerful and soothing mantra that they claimed to use while meditating. A French American woman in the group asked me if I knew the real meaning of this mantra.

I sheepishly replied that it helped keep all evil away and helped fulfill your desires. I was literally born and brought up on this mantra and never had my family explained the real meaning of this ancient mantra nor had I ever tried finding out.

The French American Woman started to speak, 'The supreme, the Divine illumination, which pervades the earth, the astral plane *(antariksha)* and the celestial *(swarga)*, is the truth and is most admirable and lovable. We meditate on that divine radiance to enlighten our intellect and awaken our spiritual wisdom.'

The strongest power is the divine power – the power of goodness, the power of a pure soul, the Brahman, the power which is untouched and can be felt deep down in the lotus of your heart. This divinity is like the glow in a light, fragrance in a flower, eternal happiness in the company of whom you love, the shade of tree on a hot sunny day, the potential music in a sitar, and the sexual fluidity on a beautiful woman.

Indeed I began practicing the real essence of achieving the divine power from that very hour on that incredible evening.

•

That magical evening in LA ignited my keen interest in the Indian spiritual texts. I began my voyage in finding the truth in the golden texts of the *Bhagavad Gita*, the Vedas and specifically the Upanishads; the writings of ancient sages and monks like Gautam Buddha, Yogi Vasishtha; modern spiritual masters like Mahatma Gandhi, Swami Vivekananda, Ralph Waldo; and the mystical verses of poets such as Kabir Das and Bhartrihari.

During this time, I began visiting various ancient sites in India. I made these trips during weekends or holidays or whenever I could just get some 'me time'. I started asking questions that I had never ever cared to ask in the last thirty-two years of my existence on this planet.

Where do I come from? Why am I here? What is the purpose of my life?

There was still time to reach the peaceful lights of illumination. Little did I know that I would come upon 'ultimate peace' at an ancient site in South India sooner than I could have imagined.

•

It was also fascinating to find the scientific relevance in these sacred texts written thousands and thousands of years ago. No one knows the authors of Vedic literature. But the knowledge seems timeless and far more advanced than any technology that exists in the modern age.

We learned in our high school science books that the whole universe (the cosmos) is being upheld due to four forces: electromagnetic, gravitational and the other two being weak and strong nuclear forces. The nuclear forces are invisible to the human eye. Even the smallest of particles, like an atom, has a nucleus around which a photon orbits at the speed of light. Interestingly, there are photons revolving around the nucleus of an atom with protons and neutrons inside. Quantum physics says that these photons are nothing but energy with no beginning or end.

Now let's look at the human body. Human beings are composed of different types of large molecules: proteins, nucleic acids, lipids, carbohydrates, etc. These molecules are held together by intermolecular forces. An example of this is the peptide bond that links amino acids together. In the 1920s, the Russian embryologist, Alexander Gurwitsch, discovered an endogenous light in the cells of the human body that proved the scientific reports of light being produced by our own cells. This forms a major component of man's inner environment and a non-material part of our bodies connecting us with the outer environment. Further experiments with state of the art modern technology in recent times suggests that all living organisms, including humans, emit a low-intensity glow that cannot be seen by the naked eye, but can be measured by photomultipliers that amplify the weak signals several million times over and enable the researchers to register it in the form of a diagram. As long as they live, cells and whole organisms give off a pulsating glow; this cellular glow is known as biophoton emission.[1]

[1.] Reference: *Macroscopic Quantum Coherence*, Proceedings of an International Conference on the Boston University, edited by Boston University and MIT, World Scientific, 1999.

Having given the insights from biochemistry, biotonogy and quantum physics above, let's look at what the Upanishads say about the universe, the cosmos and most importantly, evolution itself.

ॐ पूर्णमद: पूर्णमिदं पूर्णात् पूर्णमुदच्यते। पूर्णस्य पूर्णमादाय पूर्णमेवावशिष्यते।। ॐ शांति: शांति: शांति।।

Om Purnamadah purnamidam purnaat purnamudachyate
Purnasya purnamaday purnamevavashishyate
Om shantih shantih shantih

The great fullness or infinite is 'Brahman' – the Absolute/the universe. From fullness, nothing that is not full can come. So, what comes from fullness is fullness only. When fullness is taken from fullness, the fullness remains

– Brihadaranyaka Upanishad

I find this verse astonishingly close to the basis of evolution. A baby coming out of a mother's womb is full and when it is taken out, the mother's fullness remains. A mango tree comes from the seed of its fruit. The fruit itself has a seed that in turn contains a twenty-foot high fruit tree in a super condensed form. The egg of a hen has the making of the hen itself. When an egg comes out of a hen, the hen remains full. A small seed has a forest contained in itself and a drop of the ocean has the composition of the entire ocean. The biological information of a human being is available in the smallest form, DNA.

Upanishadic metaphysics is further elucidated in the *Madhu Vidya* (honey doctrine), where the essence of every object is described to be the same as the essence of every other object which is held to be Brahman.

As the *Shvetashvatara Upanishad* says, the Brahman is infinite. It is both near and far, both within and without every creature; it moves and is unmoving. In its subtlety, it is beyond comprehension. It is indivisible, yet appears divided in separate creatures. Know it to be the creator, the preserver, and the destroyer.

> *Dwelling in every heart, it is beyond darkness. It is called the light of lights, the object and goal of knowledge and knowledge itself. And all conscious spirit and matter both have existed since the dawn of time. They are all interconnected.*

The Upanishads say that in each of the living and nonliving organisms, there exists an illuminated energy that can neither be created nor destroyed. It is omnipresent. Are the ancient sages talking about the light energy biophoton, as we know it in modern science?

Recent research in the field of biophotons suggests that the body uses biophotons as information packages to send signals from one point to another in much the same way that fiberoptic cables transmit signals using light. Biophotons carry information about the state of the body, because healthy cells, sick cells, tumour cells and infectious viruses and bacteria have different light signals.

Now the most fascinating recent research in the field of biophotons seems to have a link with the ancient spiritual science written in the Vedic world. Advanced research in modern science suggests that biophoton emissions can be regulated by one's consciousness. The few experiments in the biophoton field indicate that human photon emission can be influenced by meditation. One such report indicated that the UPE (Biophoton emissions) changes after meditation. In subjects with high pre-meditation values, UPE decreased during meditation and remained low in the post meditation phase.[2]

I strongly feel that our ancient sages knew how to travel at the speed of light, and that brings me to the descriptions of space travelling by ancient people using their deepest meditation skills or state of 'Samadhi'. What if they knew the art of letting the consciousness enter the biophoton form of their body and then were able to travel at the speed of light outside the physical body to reach other planetary systems?

Think about it!

---

[2] Van Wijk EP, Ackerman J, Van Wijk R., *Effect of meditation on ultraweak photon emission from hands and forehead,* International Institute of Biophysics, Neuss, Germany.

Master Your Thoughts

The supreme Self is neither born nor dies, it is eternal, ever pure, indivisible and uncompounded, far beyond the senses and the ego. In him conflicts and expectations cease.He is omnipresent, beyond all thoughts.

– Atma Upanishad

When mind is detached from the senses, one reaches the summit of consciousness.
Mastery of mind leads to wisdom.
We see not the self, concealed by Maya, when the mask falls, we see the self.
Self realization is rice; all else is chaff.

– Amritabindu Upanishad

We create the world we live in by our thoughts and beliefs. Our experience of life is created directly by the way we think. Thoughts and words are powerful. Creation is made first by a thought.

All things, living or non-living, are connected in this world and beyond and with this supreme knowledge one has the power to change one's life and experiences, starting with one's thoughts. All that we are is the result of what we have thought.

If a man thinks, speaks or acts in an evil manner, pain follows him like a shadow. If a man thinks, speaks or acts in a pure manner, happiness follows him, that too like a shadow that never leaves him.

> '*At every point in time, there are infinite possibilities
> and a parallel reality exists for each possibility,
> so there are literally infinite branches.*'
> — character Daniel Jackson, TV series *Stargate*.

There are several planes of wisdom. The ancient Indian scriptures define these as seven states of enlightenment or wisdom:

- Pure intentions untouched by greed
- Self-enquiry
- A peaceful and subtle mind
- Establishment of the truth
- Total detachment
- Termination of objectivity
- Beyond all the above, a state of pure bliss and serenity.

To attain the pure bliss in our lifetime, one has to start with the mind and its mastery of thoughts.

Mid-July 2013

I took up one of the most coveted positions in the service industry. The feeling of being on the 'Indra throne' was back in my heart and I excitedly started working towards my goal with child-like passion. I wanted to do wonders for the organization;

something beyond my own individual success; I had dreams to make the brand the most admirable brand in India, connecting and serving millions of consumers. Two weeks into the role, I tried learning all about the industry, the trends and potential, as also new ideas for making us the biggest brand blockbusters.

August 2013

I said cheerfully, 'Hey Fei! How have you been? I am so happy to see you.'

I was in a meeting with one of the global managers at the company's head office. Fei Zim was in her later thirties. She was Chinese and looked like a mannequin. I used to wonder if she ever laughed in her life, and if indeed she did, how much did she charge for it!

Fei responded and she was quite expressionless, 'I am good; can we get to the update please?'

'Oh yes, of course,' I nodded, slightly embarrassed.

'So I had an absolutely amazing meeting with all the key stakeholders, partners, channel makers and as well as the team. We have loads to do and I am so, so excited!'

'Do you have a presentation?' asked Fei as stoic as ever. I immediately felt rather restless.

'Well, yes, of course! Here we go,' I said.

'What the hell? It has eighty slides!'

She jumped as though I had asked her to watch the movie *Lal Badshah* without English subtitles.

I said quickly, 'Hey don't you worry! It includes all the analytics of the Indian market and its thriving consumers, capturing the gaps that we can fill and the fresh 'green-lands' that we can create. I won't take more than one hour.'

'Kiara! We don't believe in analytics, but actions.'

I was absolutely stunned and not expecting this at all. I clarified, 'Ah! Well I agree. It's just that the strategy and actions are transcending from certain analytics which are first hand-picked from the market. The feedback is right from the consumers' mouths. It may be worth looking at the background to understand our strategy better.'

'Forget this. How are Tina and Rohit doing on the team?' Fei said dismissively.

'Tina knows her job well. She is young and just needs a little direction. Rohit is quite good in the e-commerce arena, and he is full of new ideas,' I responded in a calm tone.

'They are too junior; just f@#%ing executives. Don't give them too much authority. Balraj on that team is good. I like him,' Fei said crudely.

I was keeping calm but was absolutely flabbergasted with Fei's choice of words, 'Hey Fei, I suggest we give them some more time. I like their passion and I can coach them to grow into their roles,' I said, trying hard to put some logic into the conversation.

'F@#k them!' said Fei.

'I'm sorry?'

'What's your view on channel and distribution?' Fei abruptly changed the subject again and I for a moment wondered if she changed her car gears as well every two seconds while driving her black BMW!

'If we look at the industry sales analytics, we would realize we simply cannot ignore the distribution business and hence we need the support of the partners. How about creating business plans specifically for the top ten which will get us the majority of the pie?' I said with a straight face, closely matching Fei's mannequin looks.

'And what about website sales?' Fei asked.

'We have an excellent go-to market strategy for the same. I think we could be the top e-commerce company by the end of 2014,' I said.

'Hey…I have to leave for another meeting!' Fei said abruptly.

'But aren't we going to go through the plans and strategy?' I asked impatiently.

'No, but I will give my feedback to the India CEO,' said Fei and ended the meeting.

I reluctantly said, 'Sure. I understand.'

I wanted to kill myself. Where the hell had I landed? I started thinking aloud.

'Why the hell does she have to give the feedback to the CEO and not to me directly? What is the CEO going to do here? And feedback on what? My ass…when she hasn't even seen anything?'

I was confused and was trying to analyse my conversation with Fei like someone decoding the scans of the mummies dating back to 600 BC.

Precisely three days later, when I was back in India, I entered our small shack-like office, wearing my favourite blue outfit with a dash of gloss on my lips. I chirped good morning to all my colleagues who looked as if they had just arrived from a funereal.

I wanted to ask them if someone has died and I am sure they would have replied in a chorus, 'Yes Madam, *you*!'

Little did I know that in a few minutes, I would be wearing the same expression.

I was working on the international business plans when suddenly my phone rang; the caller was the India CEO.

'Hey Agastaya! How are you? I was about to send you an invite for the call,' I said on phone daunting my signature smile.

'I am good. How was your meeting at HO?'

'Well actually, I didn't get a chance to discuss much at the meeting; I will set up a call with Fei, according to her convenience,' I said.

'I have bad news for you Kiara. Fei called me and she was absolutely livid with the results of the meeting. She says you are not learning,' Agastaya said slowly.

Having never felt this dumb, I said. 'What? But we never discussed anything about the India strategy and plan. And learning? Where is that coming from?'

Agastaya conveniently tried to evade my questions, and said, 'Well, are you okay if certain people in your team work directly with me?'

'Of course, Agastaya. I have no problem. But I am not sure about the conversation I had with Fei. Do you want to discuss it?'

He said quickly, 'Hey, no! I have to get on a call with someone. But I think you have certainly offended her or maybe she is just insecure.'

By now I was scratching my head and thinking aloud, 'Why on earth was she insecure? I was not dating her boyfriend and she has been part of this system for a decade.'

I just replied with a blank head, 'What insecure? Oh! Okay! Let's talk when you have time. Take care. Bye!'

I kept thinking about our conversation. It was extremely odd and no matter how much I tried, I couldn't decipher the secret codes.

November 2013

I was assigned the international business and marketing portfolio due to the potential delay in the India services launch. I was enjoying every bit of my role. The quarterly sales had increased by twenty percent and our campaigns were doing exceedingly well, creating new sales benchmarks. We were coming up with newer ways of selling and at the same time, striking an emotional chord with our customers. I was extremely happy and proud of certain team members. However little did I know that, here, the words 'performance' and 'passion' just didn't matter.

Within a few weeks, I realized some petty issue or the other was taken up randomly to mortify me in front of the team; including things like why XYZ (read non-relevant person) was not marked in an email. I also realized that there were enough mischief makers in my own team who would do anything and everything to fuel the fire.

I maintained my calm and relentlessly focused on getting great results, using my trusted army of two: Rohit and Sushant who were strangely not yet diseased by the crazy virus that was infecting the entire organization. They were full of ideas which were complemented by excellent execution skills and most importantly, they were not insecure.

This 'Mr Virus' was quite interesting; it was a virus that led you to make your co-worker's life hell by getting him into trouble on every occasion; the virus that didn't let you cooperate and if did do so under rare circumstances, there was certainly a hidden agenda. It was a virus that could never see a co-worker's success as your own collective success; the virus of insecurity, jealousy and above all, dishonesty.

It seemed as if the two other companies I had worked in previously had been *swarga* and now I had been sent to this hellish world, a lower planetary system to deal with nagas and asuras! The only saving grace was the handful of good men and the fact that our campaigns and sales were doing extremely well. And we, a handful of people, would still celebrate the success and we continued to see the bigger picture.

I learned every single day about what I didn't want to become and yet I was extremely tempted to hit back and be equally nasty to the mischief makers. Thanks to my proximity to the spiritual texts, I can proudly look back and say that I had indeed mastered my thoughts by not falling prey to petty disturbances and continued to do the right things. My will to continue along the path of what was right was rock solid.

The *Chandogaya Upanishad* flashes a luminous light on the concept of 'will'.

> *Above all, a person is his will.*
> *As he wills in this life,*
> *So he becomes when he departs from it.*
> *Therefore, let your will be fixed on attaining Brahman (the supreme).*
> *Those who depart from this world without knowing who they are or what they truly desire, have no freedom here or hereafter. But those who know what they are and what they truly desire have freedom everywhere, both in this world and in the next.*

A Thursday evening
January 2014

We were sitting at our balcony of the Chennai house, overlooking a beautiful lake. Ram and I were sipping hot filter coffee and were discussing my current state of political affairs at the workplace.

Ram gave me a pleasant surprise by coming over to Chennai. Due to this current job, Nirvaan and I were in Chennai while Ram was working in Delhi.

Ram was very excited to see me. He giggled and said sweetly, 'How about another honeymoon in Kerala, but minus Nirvaan?'

While I smiled back at Ram, I started to reflect on our super adventurous relationship. We had come a long way. Nine years of stock market kind of marriage, with huge ups and downs. One thing was certain and quite hilarious that no matter how much I tried or say we tried, I still couldn't get the chemistry formula right with Ram. Whoever said that chemistry comes naturally with time, well he or she is a complete eye wash. The only thing that does come and that too in abundance is compromise and the art of being picture perfect couples. I guess most marriages work like that in this Kalayuga. Anyway, I was still lucky as Ram and I were at the least friends.

Ram suddenly broke my trail of thoughts and asked with a naughty smile, 'So my CXO wife, are you still in quest of your soulmate in me?'

I replied teasingly, 'Actually quest is still on but not in 'you', but outside of 'you'.'

Ram replied, 'Don't even try. I will kill that outsider in one shot.'

'Very funny, Ram. You won't have to do so. I am quite sorted. And for me, *tum ek hi kaafi ho*,'I started laughing loud.

My laughter was interrupted by a call on Ram's mobile, it was my mother-in-law, I heard him telling her that I was fine, and that I must be tied up in office and hence have not called back. Please talk to me directly and complain.

I waited for Ram to finish his call and said, 'Good job, buddy.' I simultaneously called my mother-in-law to apologize for not being able to take her call. She sounded alright over the call, at least.

'Anything to prevent my wife from running away,' said Ram while he took me in his arms and started to play with my hands.

Our physical proximity was further glorified with the lovely sunset. The lake view from the top floor was straight out of a painter's canvas.

I said philosophically while playing with his hair, 'If she has to run, she will. But for now she has no such plans! As a matter of fact, God has not planned anything in this area as yet.'

Ram planted a soft kiss on my cheeks and whispered in my ears, 'Even God cannot plan anything here. You are mine and only mine forever.'

Forget about our chemistry and compatibility issues, when Ram spoke like that I simply melted like strawberry ice cream. I said with a naughty smile, 'Don't so be so sure, dude.'

Later that night I decided to take an off on Friday to get away from the mindless professional riots. Ram and I decided we needed a getaway. While surfing the net, I chanced upon an ashram in Tiruvannamalai. The name of the town sounded familiar, and instantly fond memories of the beach in LA came back to me. I started to yearn for this ancient town without even realizing it. The local legends say that it's a sacred place where you can attain *moksha*.

On a Friday afternoon, we checked into the resort; the place was mystically peaceful. There was calmness in the wind, the air, and the flowers. I saw people from different walks of life and from different countries working in the place cheerfully.

After dinner, I started to think about what was going on at the work place and what should I do about it.

The corporate games were too much for me to handle; I truly didn't know what to do. All my professional values were at stake. Not only was I completely disgusted with those who were happily playing politics, but I had also been rendered speechless by the dishonesty and non-ethical behaviour of almost everyone. I found them inscrutable; I was quite close to shedding my protective ethical skin of twelve years to become disillusioned, accept the reality and become one of them; tit for tat.

And that's when I remembered what Mahatma Gandhi had once said: 'An eye for an eye only ends up making the whole world blind.' I realized that I was very close to making the same mistake as some of my colleagues. To understand them, I needed to understand their psychology and this is all I could understand: they were clearly not kind and each of their smallest moves was not towards the betterment of the organization, but to step up the corporate ladder by bringing others down.

All through my professional life, I had been inculcated with some solid values; values where the organization came first, the importance of being compassionate to my colleagues, my team members and of course my managers.

Professional compassion is about taking on another person not just as a machine, but as a human being; working together and caring for each other. An organization can have different kinds of cultures from compassion to innovation to fear to cut-throat competition. But for me, the worst culture is the culture of deceit, dishonesty and insecurity.

Two hours had passed and I had not come to any conclusions. However, I did promise myself that I would not lower myself in order to keep up with the dirty corporate games and its players.

It was around midnight, and Ram and Nirvaan were sleeping in the room. I came out of our tiny cottage which was surrounded by roses, marigolds and tulips.

I looked up into the sky and was instantly mesmerized by the beautiful stars sparkling like tiny lamps of purity and opulence. I was breathing heavily as if trying to gulp the beautiful abundance created by God. My work stress was all gone and here I was, soaking in the moments of lightness, glory, peace and contentment. There was an open air meditation cave, beautifully built with granite stones and uniquely placed in the middle of the resort. There was a seemingly supernatural quality about the cave, and my feet started moving towards it on their own. I stepped inside the open cave and looked at the heaven above; it seemed as if all the stars were trying to shower me with their light of wisdom. Without thinking too much about it, I closed my eyes and started chanting.

'Om.'

I was in a state of mind where it seemed I was going deeper into myself. It seemed like a journey of my own body; I'm not sure how much time had passed but with every chant, I felt something penetrating into the layers of my skin, bones, cells and maybe even my heart. I felt a gush of calmness because my mind was empty except for the silent vibrations of the chanting and the storm of peace accompanying my each breath. It seemed as if I was far away from time, space and the senses and was in a very different state of the world. Again, I'm not exactly sure when I felt a sudden jolt of extreme peace and gratification; the feelings cannot be described in words. I was fully conscious but there was stillness; no thoughts, just peace. I could feel myself sucked into a hole that was so bright and beautiful that I wanted to stay there forever.

The next morning at around 5.00 a.m., Ram asked sleepily, 'What on earth were you doing?'

I smiled and said, 'You have no idea, dude!'

I knew, of course, that something extraordinary had happened in that tiny cave. I felt enchanted; maybe all those years of reading spiritual texts and teachings had brought me to the moment of glory. I felt every word of the Upanishads come alive. It left me with an unprecedented feeling of peace, joy and an astonishingly pure desire to love and be compassionate. I could no more relate to any religion. I felt deep down that God was too big to be confined to any religion. I felt myself in every person I met, every plant, every animal, technically everything that I saw around me. I was appreciating every creation of God, awestruck with its vastness.

The lines from the *Isha Upanishad* were making more sense than ever before:

The Self is everywhere, the Aatman (the self) is bright, indivisible, untouched by sin, full of love, wise, immanent and transcendent. It is he who holds the cosmos together.

When a big change occurs in your life, it forces you to change paths. Sometimes, the new path is not easy and sometimes even looks exceptionally difficult.

For me, to leave my present organization was a tough decision. But after experiencing ultimate peace, it was much easier to trust the flow of life. I was absolutely certain that the new path that had opened before me contained experiences that I would never have been able to gain otherwise.

When we look back at negative events that occurred in the past, we often realize that there was something miraculously positive in it and how it in fact, transformed our lives forever. Random events when connected together bring us to a life we would never change for anything.

To this day, only a rare few have had the experience of seeing the true light of life. The biggest wisdom is self-realization. The self is hidden in the deepest caves of the heart; just like a biophoton which is emanating light from our body cells is seated deep inside the atom. We cannot see the consciousness through our five senses, but can only realize it deep within with a still mind and a pure heart.

Says Ralph Waldo Emerson, an American essayist, lecturer, and poet who led the Transcendentalist Movement in the mid-19th century:

What lies behind us
and what lies before us
Are tiny matters compared to
What lies within us.

In the *Bhagavad Gita,* there is a verse that tells us about the magnificent powers of mind control to the extent where you can realize God with a still and pure mind.

Some realize the Self within them through the practice of meditation; some by the path of wisdom and others by selfless service. Others may not know these paths; but listening to and following the instructions of an illumined teacher, they too go beyond death.

The most important step towards self-liberation is mastering your thoughts. What you are is a bundle of your imagination in the present moment. It's very easy to say who has got the time to keep filtering thoughts, but believe me, once you jump start this process of retaining the positive thoughts and letting go of the negative thoughts, within no time you will realize that your mind is now your slave and not vice versa. You should be controlling and mastering your mind and not the other way around. In each one of us, there is a supreme power that can control each little electrical circuit in our mind.

It took me time to come to this point of self-liberation. I truly realize that the mind is a tricky place and also a fabulous lawyer; it has all the arguments to trash an otherwise beautiful moment and seeds of happiness.

❤ *Mind-mastery is the stepping stone to life management.*

The one who conquers the mind, goes beyond the basic foundation of his identity which is 'I'. He is able to look and feel the realms of ultimate happiness that comes with a pure heart and mind. This realm is the higher state of enlightenment where each of the doer's action is channelized towards conquering the illusions *(maya)* and attraction *(moh)* of all kinds, where all desires succumb and only pure state of love and compassion exists in harmony with one's own self. The completeness of a being is beyond the physical body. In one of the ancient Indian scriptures, where Yoga Vasishtha is imparting supreme knowledge to Lord Rama, there is a verse that beautifully explains the mind's role in creating the several births and several experiences in a lifetime. It says that it is the mind that creates the physical body by mere thoughts, just as a potter makes a pot. It creates new bodies and brings about the destructions of what exists, and all this by a mere wish. When a mind wants to see diversity, he sees mindless diversities. When he wants to see the truth, he only see the pure consciousness in one and all.

If you take a moment to reflect on your own life, you will realize that you create your own life using your imagination, thoughts and actions at any given point in time. When the mind is controlled like a slave, you control the trigger of absolute reality – the reality which is peaceful, serene, and full of joy and compassion.

February 2014

It is a hot and sunny afternoon in the month of February 2014. I was sitting on a brand new chair – there were still bits of polythene on the handgrip. Around me was a group of twenty-five odd animated colleagues. Amidst total chaos, I was in total harmony – in peace, and filled with undiluted calmness and experiencing a nearly silent mind.

The day had finally arrived when I was to resign from one of the most coveted corporate positions in the country. In hindsight, the year leading up to this day had undoubtedly been the best time of my life. I don't say this about my professional life, but in every little sense about my spiritual one. Life is a bucket full of experiences; some are strange, some enthralling, and some just leave you gasping for breath.

These experiences of a lifetime made me, in simple words, a much better person than I had ever been. I love my new avatar which is much closer to the real 'me'. The magnificent writings from ancient Indian sages call it 'satya' or the truth.

I, Kiara Seth, a thirty-three-year-old corporate honcho was about to fly – not to another level or a bigger brand, but to take the biggest flight of my life. I had realized the purpose of my life, and with folded hands, I had surrendered myself to the supreme truth.

Later in the evening, I picked Nirvaan from day care. On our way home, Nirvaan excitedly told me about how he had helped his friend Nilesh in copying notes from the blackboard. Nilesh was in Nirvaan's class and had recently gone through a complicated eye surgery.

He asked me sweetly if it counts as good karma.

I proudly replied, with tears rolling down my cheeks, 'Indeed, my love! Add it to your account!'

Nirvaan asked, 'But why are you crying?'

And I replied emotionally, 'They're happy tears. Who says life doesn't come full circle? Ask me! Tell every friend of yours about the good karma bank. Let them open their respective accounts immediately. *After all, it doesn't hurt to be nice.*'

It was midnight, and as usual, my inner self started to think of all that had happened so far in my life. I decided to put together my experiences and learning in a form that could reach and benefit thousands of others.

I think I know the purpose of my life in a more concrete manner than ever before. My purpose is to be a better human being. I had promised God that I would give, be kind, be compassionate and would pursue the path of truthfulness. I had also promised to relentlessly try to attain the power of the infinite, the power of fullness, and ultimately the boon to break from the cycle of birth and death.

March 2014

I was taking a walk around the lake just outside my apartment complex in Chennai. I had no clue what was next in my professional and personal life when my thoughts were interrupted by a call on my mobile. The call was from Canada.

The voice on the other side spoke, 'Hello, is that Kiara?'

'Yes this is Kiara. How can I help you?'

'Well, we were wondering if you would like to explore a global marketing role with us. We are a multinational based in Canada...'

The person spoke for almost fifteen minutes explaining the role and the company.

'Yes, I am interested,' I said thinking and analyzing at the same time.

The call ended on an extremely positive note.

I looked up and smiled excitedly. I don't know whom I was smiling at, but it was a natural rejoinder. I thanked God instantly. I was happy to believe in my faith in the Supreme Being, one who is omnipresent, full of love, indivisible, pure, the source of supreme light, untouched, beyond all bondages, serene, invisible but the strongest. I reminded myself that career, fame, money – everything is immaterial. The only truth is the Lord of supreme love and I would love and only love to be a better human being with each passing moment of my lifetime. And there is someone up there to take care of me, no matter what...only if I am truly and deeply nice.

As I Promised God

As I promise to help
As I promise to give
As I promise to live every moment
As I promise to tread only one path
The path of truth and only truth
As I promise to give thanks for everything and anything
As I promise to carry the attitude of gratitude

As I inspire
And not conspire
As I smile and make everyone smile
As I create new life and help it grow
As I try not to destroy any being

As I make myself proud
Not just by degrees or by rank or by money
But by good deeds and spreading joy all around
As I consider all equal
No matter who
As I promise not to fear
No matter what happens

As I believe in myself and every life on this planet
As I promise to be kind
As I realize that good deeds never die
As I only spread energy that is positive
As I love and only love above all
As I try to reach 'the infinite' inside me, I promise God to be a better human being with each passing day.

●

Thank you from the bottom of my heart for your precious time.
May God Bless You.

Upcoming title from the same author

Love is Simple
...but why are men so complex!

Lavanya Sharma is born in the wrong time, it seems. For she is charming, very beautiful, kind-hearted and a good human being. Yet, she fares miserably in the area of finding her true love.

From adolescence, to mid-twenties, to early thirties - Lavanya has tried hard to find her soul mate. To her, there is that one special person who is made just for her, and she is sure she will find him. But how would she know if this is the one? Hit and trial, perhaps!

At each stage of her quest (or we may say, with each man that she tries to find her soul mate in), she realizes how complex men are in the areas of love and understanding. From boys who run at the merest mention of commitment, to those who don't have the guts to stand up for their feelings; from men who promise to offer her the world, to that one who is indeed her world – her sometimes hilarious and at times dramatic experiences make us realize that love is the most profound and pure feeling on this planet, an eternal alignment of two people's mind, body and heart. It is simple, and yet we make it so complicated.

Amisha Sethi is an executive scholar from Kellogg School of Management, Northwestern University, Chicago, and holds an MBA degree in Marketing from Amity Business School. She was awarded the "Young women rising star" at World Women Leadership Congress 2014 and has won numerous awards and recognition in her corporate life. Along with holding top notch positions in leading companies in the past thirteen years, she has also done extensive research in ancient scriptures. In this book, she uses certain hilarious, dramatic and enthralling experiences of a young girl to understand the ultimate purpose of life — to be a better human with each passing day.

Write to Amisha at
reach@amishasethi.com,
or visit *www. amishasethi.com*

She would love to know about your nice deeds and views!

Join the 'Nice Gang' at
www.facebook.com/amishasethiauthor